GOLDEN

Mage

OTHER BOOKS BY DOROTHY DREYER

Phoenix Descending

Paragon Rising

Cauldron of Ash

Christmas in Silverwood

THE EMPIRE OF THE LOTUS SERIES

Crimson Mage

Copper Mage

Golden Mage

Emerald Mage

Sapphire Mage

Amethyst Mage

Diamond Mage

GOLDEN

Mage

EMPIRE OF THE LOTUS

BOOK THREE

DOROTHY DREYER

Golden Mage
Empire of the Lotus Book Three
Second edition

Paperback ISBN: 978-1-948661-43-0

Published May 2020 by Snowy Wings Publishing
PO Box 1035, Turner, OR 97392

*For my family, because we're on
lockdown together and
haven't killed each other*

Haunted by evil. Bound by prophecy. Driven by faith.

Consumed by his doomed love for the empress Lakshmi, Kashmeru will stop at nothing to break the spell that has kept him locked in a hidden tomb. With the comet Akutake fast approaching, the clock is ticking for the elite mages to gather and fight Kashmeru's shadow army and the mysterious and powerful dark mages.

As Mayhara, Jae, and Shiro race to acquire the arcane daggers before they fall into the wrong hands, Huojin and Salina must face their destinies as golden mages and learn to harness their power to destroy the enemy—before the enemy destroys them first.

*For gold is tried in the fire
and acceptable men in the furnace
of adversity.*
—George Santayana

The legend goes …

*The ancient deity Kashmeru knew only one true love—
the Lotus empress Lakshmi, who in his eyes possessed all
beauty and grace the universe could hold. Their hearts
called to one another, a hold so strong that neither one
could deny the bond. But Lakshmi knew that
Kashmeru's spirit was not pure, for an evil dwelled
within his soul, a wickedness so corrupt that it could
destroy the universe.*

*And when she denied him her love, destroying the
universe was the very thing he vowed to do.*

*Throughout the centuries, their reincarnations were
drawn to one another, but the outcome was always the
same: Lakshmi would never give Kashmeru her heart.*

*To put an end to his constant chase, the Empire of the
Lotus defeated Kashmeru and sealed him in a tomb
using mage powers, where he would remain trapped …*

*… until the Council of the Seven could secure the blood
of the Lotus empress to set him free.*

THE SEVEN HOUSES OF MAGES

Crimson: earth, stability, survival, security.

Copper: water, ice, pleasure, guilt.

Golden: fire, willpower, shame.

Emerald: air, wind, heart, love, grief.

Sapphire: throat, sound, truth, lies.

Amethyst: vision, sight, illusions, secrets.

Diamond: spirituality, emotion, virtue, integrity.

One

Salina pushed aside the gauze curtain and gazed out at the koi pond. The clouds had parted enough to allow some beams of sun to dance upon the water. She took a deep breath in through her nose and released it through rounded lips, attempting to clear her mind and ease her tensed muscles. She'd hardly slept, keeping vigil over Huojin as she lay wounded and suffering in her bed at the temple.

The newscaster on the televiewer caught her attention when he mentioned the Akutake comet. Turning away from the window, Salina tucked a golden-brown curl behind her ear and grabbed the controller, turning up the volume a bit. A petite woman with short, brunette hair tilted her head slightly at the camera. In the corner of the screen, a still image of the oncoming comet was displayed.

"This is Akutake's second cycle through our solar system, the last one—182 years ago—bringing it roughly twelve million kilometers away from Earth. Astrophysicists at the New United Asian Space Agency predict the comet will come exceptionally closer this year, approximating the proximity to be a mere seven million kilometers from Earth. Its closest range will align with the air space above the city of New Delhi in India's district of New United Asia in less than a month.

"Though NUASA reassures us the comet does not impose a risk, a movement of the devout population across New India, between New Jaipur and New India, has encouraged citizens to offer greetings to Akutake in the form of prayers, meditation, and festivals honoring the comet. Because of this, the governor of New Jaipur has arranged a number of

festivals to welcome the comet in its various phases of approach, beginning with the Navratri Festival, taking place next week."

A rustling of sheets made Salina turn. With a furrowed brow and a hiss through her teeth, Huojin stirred. Her dark hair was damp and clung to her temples. She wasn't able to move too much, with half her body covered in severe burns. Though Huojin would have been best treated at a hospital's burn center, it was too risky. Mages were outlawed, and walking into a medical facility, which would no doubt be occupied by Imperial Police, would mean certain imprisonment. Or worse.

Jae had acquired the help of a doctor who was willing to keep his mouth shut for compensation. The doctor had provided burn creams and ointments, dressing Huojin's wounds to the best of his ability with what little resources he could provide. Left with pain pills and instructions on how to change her bandages, the mages were on their own to help Huojin to heal. Only time would tell if it would be enough.

Luckily, Huojin's fire powers drew most of the heat from the burns, converting the element into vapers that were released into the air. The result was a very humid room.

Salina hurried to Huojin's side. Huojin's eyes opened a fraction of an inch, her gaze resting upon Salina.

"Sal—" Huojin's raspy voice was cut short by harsh coughing. She winced as the coughing fit jolted her body.

"Take it easy." Salina's voice was gentle as she reached for a washcloth on the side table. She dunked the washcloth in the small basin of water before gently dabbing at the sweat beaded on Huojin's forehead. It was one of the only places not burned by Naree's fire magic.

"Where… Where is everyone?" Huojin asked, her face still contorted from the pain. "What happened with Darshana? Is she okay?"

"Don't worry about that right now. You need to heal before you can deal with anything else."

"But is she alive?"

"Yes. But she hasn't woken up yet."

It had been a series of harried events since the battle with Naree and the Pishacha. Huojin's injuries had been the worst of them all, but Darshana had been hurt even before the battle had begun, and she had yet to awaken.

"I need some water," Huojin said, shifting slightly to

sit up.

Salina poured her a glass from the pitcher on the side table. "Here."

"I can't remember everything," Huojin said as she took the glass. She winced as she sipped, and then she handed the glass back to Salina. "I remember the fire. I remember Naree and the Pishacha disappearing. And you bringing me to the car. But I must have passed out from the pain."

Salina released a shuddered breath, feeling the panic as if it were happening all over again. She pushed through the feeling and focused on the events that had followed. "We brought you here. Jae got a doctor to bandage you up."

"I think I remember that. It felt like a dream. A really… agonizing dream."

"He gave you a shot of morphine and left us some pills. But Shiro said he knows of a witch who could heal you better than any doctor could."

Huojin scoffed. "A witch?"

"Yeah." Salina gave her a half-shrug. "Unfortunately, he can't remember how to find her, and Mayhara thought it was too risky for him to wander off searching for her.

He said we'd have to wait for Darshana to come to. If she ever does."

"Didn't the doctor help her?"

Salina stood and began pacing. "Yes, of course. He tended to her injury but couldn't do anything more. He couldn't be certain if she would remain unconscious or not without a scan. But since we can't take her to a hospital…"

"We can't do anything but wait." Huojin shifted again, drawing in a breath through her teeth.

"What do you need?" Salina rushed back to Huojin's side. "What can I do?"

"Maybe those pain meds?"

Salina didn't waste any time. She quickly uncapped the bottle of pills and slipped two capsules into Huojin's bandaged hand. Huojin slid them into her mouth and took the glass Salina offered her.

As Huojin leaned back against her pillow again, Salina felt a heavy weight on her heart. She hated seeing her best friend like this. Huojin had been her saving grace when Salina had arrived at the mage academy, taking her under her wing. She'd been there for her whenever she had needed someone, which Salina had often needed, being so far away from her own country. And she'd been her personal mentor during golden mage training, especially when Darshana had been too busy to advise her. She was her home away from home, the one who'd comforted her when her mother had died and had paid for her ticket home, and Salina would do anything for her.

To see her suffering like this was killing Salina.

"Are the pills helping any?"

Huojin squirmed, her face twisted in pain. "Not yet. I think I need a distraction. Talk to me about something."

"What should I talk about?" Salina steadied her breath, fighting off tears.

"Anything pleasant. Tell me about your home."

"Massawa was originally a small, seaside village. It extended over the same area as the Kingdom of Axum, which used to be called the Kingdom of Zuma. It has the oldest mosque in Africa—the Mosque of the Companions—which is believed to be the first mosque on the African continent."

"So it's old," Huojin said with the hint of a smirk on her lips.

Salina smiled, relishing in the fact that her friend still

had her sense of humor. "Very old."

Huojin licked her lips and swallowed hard, her eyes drifting halfway closed. "Tell me more."

"It is very hot in Massawa. There's not a lot of rain. Like, ever. It's famous for having very high summer humidity despite being a desert city. The desert heat and the high humidity together make it seem unbearably hot. But the sky is gorgeous. It's always clear and bright throughout the year."

"What about the food?" Huojin asked. "I bet the food is divine."

"I think it is." Salina laughed. "But my absolute favorite is anything with *hilbet*. It's like a paste made from lentils and fava beans. I remember coming home after grade school and my mother would already be preparing dinner. She'd make a stew called *tsebhi* and flatbread and *hilbet*. And I would always eat the most *hilbet*, which made my brother mad."

"Yeah, that sounds like you." Huojin smiled at her. "It sounds lovely. I wish I could visit there."

"You can one day. I promise. I'll take you there myself."

Huojin's smile widened. Her thin wisps of black

lashes almost entirely blocked the view of her chestnut brown eyes. "Tell me more."

"Well, even though it's called the Red Sea, it is the bluest of blues you'd ever see." She let her head fall back as she recalled her youth. "I remember going to the shore with my family when no one had to work or go to school. Those were the best days. They were precious to us. We didn't have a lot of money, but we felt rich because of the love our family had for each other."

When Salina looked back at Huojin, her eyes were closed, and a small smile rested on her lips. Her slow, steady breathing told Salina she'd fallen asleep.

Salina stood, her heart feeling compressed with worry. It wasn't so long ago that she had lost her mother. She wouldn't be able to bear it if she lost her best friend too.

Two

Mayhara adjusted her eyes to the darkness of the old shop. It wasn't that it didn't have any lighting inside; it was more as if the shop owners were relying on the bright sunlight coming in through the windows to illuminate the shop. The only problem was it was a partly cloudy day, and the sconces in the shop were merely faint yellow glimmers on the walls. The place smelled like metal and paper, and

Mayhara distinctly heard the ripping sound of a buzz saw buzzing coming from behind the far wall.

Jae, who had ventured deeper into the store than she had, studied a few of the scrolls on the dusty shelves before nodding at her. They were in the right place. Now they just had to speak to the right people.

Jae spread his gaze around the shop, running a hand through his dark hair and then over the hint of stubble at his jaw. Mayhara noticed his eyes flit to the upper corners of the space.

He's checking for cameras.

Adjusting the dark blue scarf that covered her long, silky, black hair, Mayhara followed Jae across the red-tiled floor. He headed toward the mahogany counter, where a woman in a flowered, green *cheongsam* dress and a man in a black *tangzhuang* jacket stood. They appeared to be ordinary workers, probably a decade older than Mayhara and Jae, neatly groomed with a graceful manner in the way they moved. Mayhara worried that they might not have any information about the scrolls she and Jae had stolen.

Jae approached and bowed to them. The young woman looked him up and down, her brows drawn down. Jae glanced back at Mayhara for a moment.

"May I help you?" the man behind the counter asked. His smile seemed genuine.

"I've passed by this shop a few times but never came in here. It's charming." Jae gave him a nod.

"Thank you," the man answered. The woman remained quiet, her face hard to read.

Mayhara sidled up beside Jae.

"How long have you been working here?" Jae asked.

"For as long as I can remember," the man answered.

"Ten years," the woman said, her hand planted on her hip.

"But we practically grew up in the shop," the man said. "I learned to walk right over there. Nearly destroyed a shelf of vases."

Jae let out a small laugh along with the man's throaty chuckle. The woman remained stoic.

"So, you're part of the family who owns the shop?" Jae asked.

The woman crossed her arms, her lips in a straight line. When Jae met her gaze, her eyes went to the counter as she adjusted her *fa-zan* hairpin.

The male tilted his head slightly and studied Jae for a

quick moment. His eyes then flit over to Mayhara. "Is there something in particular you're curious about?"

"I'm sorry." Jae pressed his palms together and bowed. "I don't mean to be rude. My name is Jae, and this is my friend May—" Mayhara and Jae exchanged glances momentarily. They couldn't be sure the shop workers would recognize Mayhara from police bulletins stating she was wanted for murder. Better not to give them her real name. "Maya."

"Nice to meet you," Mayhara said.

After a short pause, the man gave them a slight bow. "I'm Nian, and this is my sister, Zhen."

Zhen made a quick movement Mayhara didn't quite catch, and Nian responded by letting out a muffled *oomph* and reaching for his lower leg. Mayhara bit back her urge to laugh, knowing Zhen must have kicked him. Perhaps she didn't want people knowing her name.

"Your family's scrolls are beautiful," Jae said.

Nian cleared his throat. "Thank you."

"Have you learned the art of scroll making, or are your duties strictly to manage the shop?"

Nian glanced at Zhen, as if unsure to continue speaking freely.

"It is a family business," Zhen said. "And as such, we must learn every aspect."

Jae nodded.

"Would you be able to tell your scrolls from others?" Mayhara asked.

"Of course." Zhen lifted her chin. "It would be a dishonor not to be at least somewhat of an expert on the subject of the family business."

"The reason we ask is because we're looking for some information on a couple scrolls. They appear to be from your company." Mayhara swung her canvas bag forward and retrieved the scroll tubes, laying them on the counter.

Zhen rested her hand on her chest, just below her throat, and stepped closer to her brother. Nian's gaze went between Mayhara and Jae before gently placing his fingers upon the end of one tube. With narrowed eyes, he slipped the scroll from the first tube and turned it over in his hand. He held it at an arm's distance as he unrolled it. As he studied it, Zhen looked up at Mayhara, her mouth in a straight line.

"This one looks familiar." Nian spoke slowly. Deliberately. "But the digitalization tells me it was made in connection with an outsourcing company that installs the software for this type."

"You wouldn't be able to tell us what or who those lights are assigned to?" Mayhara asked.

"Not without getting the coding documents from the digitalizing company." Nian rolled up the scroll and stuck it in its tube.

"Can you take a look at the other scroll?" Jae asked.

Nian breathed in deeply through his nose. He didn't seem irritated, and Mayhara wondered if he had something to be afraid of. Paranoia scraped at her skin as she wondered if Nian and Zhen might have in fact recognized her after all. She watched their hands, making sure they weren't tripping some emergency call button that might alert the Imperial Police. Had they already called for them? Were Nian and Zhen just biding their time until the authorities arrived?

Mayhara instinctively looked toward the window, fidgeting with her head scarf as Nian opened the other scroll. His brow wrinkled, and he blinked a couple times as he scanned the scroll.

Zhen pursed her lips and backed away. "We don't recognize this one."

Nian swiveled his head her way and began whispering

in harsh tones in Mandarin. Zhen argued back.

Mayhara didn't understand their words, but she recognized the sound of it. She turned to Jae, wondering if he knew the language.

"They're arguing about whether or not they should help us," Jae said, loud enough for the two siblings to hear him. "She's telling him she doesn't trust us."

"Trust has to be earned," Zhen suddenly interjected. Her hands were balled into fists. "There are wars taking place no one knows about, no one could even dream about, and you don't get to decide if we are pulled into them or not."

Nian placed a gentle hand on her arm and said something to her in calming tones. Zhen crossed her arms and backed away from him but didn't argue further.

Squaring his shoulders, Nian tilted his head slightly. "Could you, perhaps, state your motivation for wanting to find the meaning of this scroll?"

Jae leaned closer over the counter and lowered his voice. "We know of these wars. Believe me. We are a part of them. We are mages, the loyal warriors of the Empire of the Lotus."

Zhen and Nian stared at them for a moment. The

only sound that could be heard was their breathing.

"Mages are outlawed," Zhen said. "It is illegal for us to help you."

Nian turned quickly to his sister. "Where do your loyalties lie, sister? We have always served the empire. The Lotus has always been our sovereign goddess."

Zhen jutted out her chin. "My loyalties would lie with the empress, of course. But there has been no news of her rebirth."

"It's been kept secret," Jae told her. "It's the one hundredth reincarnation, and according to the prophecy, the Lotus is in danger. Her reincarnation has been kept secret to protect her from the Pishacha."

Nian and Zhen exchanged glances, and then Nian dropped his gaze. Jae raised his hand, and his palm began to glow a bright blue. Zhen's eyes widened and her bottom lip trembled.

"I have a feeling this doesn't surprise you," Jae said to Nian. The blue glow grew, illuminating Nian's face.

"We have heard about her reemergence, yes. But only recently."

Zhen swallowed hard.

Mayhara pushed back her head scarf. "And you

understand this is the one-hundredth reincarnation?"

Nian nodded.

"If you honor the Lotus, we need your help," Jae said. "Kashmeru has his shadow army out, and they already have the Lotus in their grasp. She's under his spell."

Zhen's jaw dropped. "We are doomed, then. We've already lost."

"No." Mayhara laid her hands flat on the counter. "That's what the mages are for. We're going to rescue her. We have the power to fight the Pishacha. But we need all the help we can get. Our guru says this scroll is one of the keys that will turn things in our favor."

Zhen turned to Nian and spurted out something in Mandarin again. She shook her head at her brother, but he calmly reached out to stop her from flailing her arms as he spoke to her. Mayhara didn't have to understand the language to know Nian wanted to help them, despite his sister's protests.

Zhen let out a huff and took a step back, placing a hand on her hip and almost pouting at Mayhara and Jae.

"Will you take another look?" Mayhara asked, this time directly to Nian. "Maybe something on it looks familiar to you?"

"We think it's a map," Jae said. "But we can't tell what location it might be."

Nian pulled the scroll closer and took a better look, running his hand along the material.

"It's very old," Nian said. "The paper is different from the modern kind we use today. There are some smudges in the ink, almost as if someone made this in a hurry."

Mayhara and Jae waited patiently as Nian followed a few of the ink markings with his fingers. After what seemed like a long while, Nian looked up at them.

"I'm sorry," he said. "That's all I can tell you at this point. I can speak with some older family members. Perhaps they can be of better assistance."

Zhen began yelling in Mandarin, but Nian shouted back, silencing her.

"Can we keep the scroll here so that I may show one of them?" Nian asked.

"I don't think that's a good idea." Jae rolled up the scroll and put it back in its tube. "I can leave you a number to call when you've found someone who might be able to help. We can come back."

"It's also for your safety," Mayhara said. "If the Pishacha come looking for this, you could be in danger."

"That's the first sensible thing you've said," Zhen mumbled under her breath.

Mayhara ignored Zhen's comment and nodded to Nian. "Thank you for your help."

A buzzing from Jae's pocket forced him to turn away. He and Mayhara stepped away from the counter as he checked the screen of his Linq.

With a quick glance at Mayhara, Jae held his Linq to his ear. "Shiro?"

Mayhara waited for a second.

"Okay, we're on our way." Jae swiftly tucked the Linq away.

Mayhara searched his face. "What is it?"

"It's Darshana. She's awake."

Three

Naree stood on her balcony, overlooking the gardens. The villa was quiet, and all she wanted to do was breathe in the tranquility and sip her tea. The last few weeks had been a struggle. There were times when she was unsure of what she was doing, like she was living a dream. And there were times when she felt as if her mind was separated from her body, when she could see what actions she'd been carrying out but had no control over them.

Because of him.

She took a deep breath and looked upward. Birds danced in the air, circling each other as they soared across the sky. She breathed in, the scent of her rooibos tea mixing with the smell of fresh spring flowers in the gardens. She allowed herself to close her eyes. A memory from another life began to play out in her mind.

She stirred her tea, a soft breeze playing with the hem of her skirt as she sat at an outdoor table at her favorite cafe. He approached the table. His thick, black hair was a bit longer now, the ends extending enough to tuck behind his ears. His dark brows gave a strong contrast to the tiny flecks of silver in his anthracite gray eyes. His smile lit up his face, and when he took her hand to place a kiss upon it, she blushed.

"My love," he said as he slid into the seat across from her. "This is the highlight of my day. You are an absolute vision of beauty."

"As are you," she replied with a sheepish smile.

He laughed. "You find me beautiful?"

"Yes, I do." She leaned forward and filled the cup in

front of him with tea.

He continued to smile at her as he sipped, watching her face.

She narrowed her eyes. "What is it?"

"I'm sorry. I don't know what you mean." Still, his grin did not fade.

"Something is up. I can tell."

He tilted his head. "I should have known better than to try to hide something from you."

"What are you hiding?"

He set down his teacup. "I was going to wait until this evening, after our stroll through the park."

"Now you must tell me," she insisted.

"I suppose I have no choice."

She giggled. "You don't."

"Very well, then." He reached into his trousers pocket and pulled out a rectangular, black, velvet box.

Her eyes widened as he set it on the table and slid it closer to her.

"For me?"

"My love, everything I have and everything I am is for you."

She practically swooned at his words.

"Open it," he said. His smile was child-like.

She almost danced in her seat from excitement. The box was soft under her touch. When she opened it, her breath caught in her throat. Inside was a shiny gold chain-link necklace, a tiny charm of a dove in flight sitting in its center.

"It's lovely," she exclaimed. "But why? What occasion could it be that I deserve such a gift?"

"The occasion—" he stood and took the necklace from the box. "—that I am utterly and completely in love with you."

A flutter in her stomach caused her to fiddle with her blouse. With a feather-light touch, he swept her dark brown hair off her neck, draping it over her shoulder. He placed the necklace around her neck, his fingers softly brushing against her bare skin as he closed the clasp. She gasped as the cold metal of the charm touched her chest.

His hands rested on her shoulders. "Do you love it?

She ran her fingers over the gold as she stood and turned to face him. "I do."

He placed his hands on her waist and urged her closer. "Do you love me?"

Their gazes locked. She reached up and traced a finger along his cheek and down to his jaw. He leaned down and gently pressed his lips against hers, his hands slipping behind her to pull her even closer. She deepened the kiss, letting him take what he desired, letting his passion fill her with want.

It felt so right, yet…

She gasped and pulled away. Her hands flew to her lips.

"My love?" He searched her face. "What's wrong?"

Fear filled her. His eyes now appeared black as coal. There was a presence within him, something sinister that loomed like a dark cloud, a shadow that chased away the light.

Evil.

Deep inside, Kashmeru lurked. His evil is what she felt radiating off him. But she couldn't say it.

She took two more steps back. His brow furrowed.

"No." A scowl began to form on his face. "Do not cast me away."

She shook her head and backed away even more. "I… We… We can't. This. This is wrong."

Before he had a chance to object, she turned and ran.

"Your Highness."

Naree turned to find Bhutano standing by the sliding doors of the balcony, his hands clasped behind his back and his uniform crisp and wrinkle-free.

"Yes?" She stirred her tea, which she knew had to have gone cold by now.

"The dark mages are ready to accompany you. We need to find the next dagger." He gestured toward the door, indicating she should follow. "Time is closing in on us."

She sighed, leaving her cold tea behind on the balcony railing. "All right. Let's go."

Four

Mayhara's heart pounded the whole way back to the temple. Though she was relieved to hear Darshana had awoken from her coma-like sleep, she needed more information. Was Darshana coherent? Was she in pain? Impatience tore at her so much, she nearly yelled at Jae to ignore the speed restrictions and drive his motorcycle faster. Instead, she forced herself to practice the breathing techniques

Darshana had taught her to keep her calm.

Wind whipped at her face, but the sound of the motorcycle's motor was cloaked under Jae's sound magic. Under the stifling press of her helmet, she felt hot, the anxiety of needing to see Darshana causing her to sweat.

Once they reached the carport of the temple, Mayhara hastily tore off her helmet and dismounted Jae's bike. She could hear Jae struggling to keep up with her.

Jae called out to her to slow down, but she hardly acknowledged his words. She needed to know Darshana was okay. Somehow, she felt as if it would be a bad omen for their mission if Darshana wasn't all right.

Mayhara rounded corners and skidded down halls until she reached Darshana's room. The door was open, and both Shiro and Salina turned to her as she entered. On the bed, propped up with pillows, lay Darshana. Her eyes were closed, fine lines settled above her cheeks and lips, and her long, white hair fanned out over her pillows.

Mayhara's heart sank. "I thought she was awake."

"I *am* awake." Darshana opened her eyes a fraction of an inch. "Can't an old woman rest her eyes without the world thinking she's dead and gone?"

Despite herself, Mayhara laughed. This brought

smiles to both Shiro's and Salina's faces.

Mayhara hurried to Darshana's side. "We're so relieved you're awake. We thought—"

"Never mind what you thought. I taught you not to dwell on the negative, didn't I?"

Mayhara bowed her head, her gaze staying on the guru. "Yes, of course."

"Do you need anything?" Salina asked, stepping forward and attempting to adjust Darshana's pillows.

Darshana waved away her efforts. "First of all, stop fussing over me. Second, I need you to tell me exactly what happened with Naree and the Pishacha."

Jae suddenly appeared in the doorway. "Darshana."

Darshana let out a deep breath. "Yes, yes. I'm fine. My dears, time is of the essence. What happened in the battle with Naree?"

Everyone began speaking at once, and Darshana's expression showed she was having trouble keeping track of who was saying what.

"They somehow found us when we left the warehouse."

"Naree created a cave in the middle of the road."

"She said she wanted the dagger."

"We fought inside the cave."

"Not only the Pishacha there, but others."

"Mages."

"Dark mages. Like the one we saw on the bridge."

"They fought alongside her."

"But we matched them in might, and they disappeared."

"But not before Naree unleashed a firestorm on Huojin."

"She's badly burned."

This last part made Darshana sit up. Everyone was quiet for a moment.

Salina looked around at everyone, then put a hand on Darshana's arm. "The doctor who tended to you treated her as well. He did everything he could."

Darshana swiped strands of hair away from her face. "Where is she?"

When Darshana threw back her covers, Mayhara protested.

"No. Don't get up," she said.

"She's resting," Salina told her. "She's healing, though."

Darshana shook her head. "I want to see her. I need

to put my hands on her to see what's going on inside."

Mayhara and Jae exchanged glances.

Shiro sighed and took a step back, nodding. He pushed his copper-streaked, dark hair off his forehead, averting his gaze.

"All right," Jae said. "Just… take it easy."

They gathered around her as if she were the most fragile thing in the world until she scowled and waved them away, mumbling about minding people's personal space. Huojin's room wasn't far down the hall, but Darshana was still breathing heavily once they got there.

It had been a couple days since Mayhara had seen Huojin. She knew the elite golden mage needed rest and time to heal, and Mayhara had been busy helping Jae track down the scroll maker's shop. Looking at her now, Mayhara's heart hurt. Some of Huojin's burns seemed to have healed, but blackened, blistering skin still covered a good portion of Huojin's body.

Darshana pursed her lips as she approached the bed where Huojin lay sleeping. Closing her eyes, the guru reached out toward Huojin. Her hands came so close to the golden mage, one would think she was actually touching her. Darshana moved her hands over the space above Huojin's skin, now and then wincing as if feeling Huojin's pain. Everyone remained quiet, waiting for her to finish her analysis.

At long last, Darshana pulled her hands back and opened her eyes. She turned to the group, her mouth in a straight line. "She's healing, but not as fast as I'd like."

"Is there something we can do to help her?" Salina's brow was creased with worry.

Before Darshana could answer, Shiro spoke up. "I was thinking maybe the swamp witch could help her. The same way she helped me. I'm sure she must have something that could heal Huojin's burns."

Darshana nodded. "Yes. I think she might. Amalia's understanding of mage powers would be beneficial in providing the perfect tincture or salve needed to help the healing process along."

"Can we trust this Amalia?" The deep voice from the doorway made them all turn.

Mayhara had almost forgotten that the Sacred Key had been staying with them at the temple. Darshana narrowed her eyes at the man with slicked-back, salt-and-pepper hair, taking in his white, button-down shirt and dress pants. She hadn't been aware of his presence.

They'd never had the chance to tell her about him before she'd been injured and fallen into her coma-like sleep.

The Sacred Key bowed. "I'm sorry to interrupt."

"It's okay," Jae said to Darshana. "This is Mr. Kitaro. He's the Sacred Key I located using the scroll."

"It is a pleasure to meet you, Guru Darshana. I've heard great things about you."

She bowed in return but still did not smile. "Sacred Keys are connected to Lotus empresses of the past. I must assume you are related to the late Anjana Patel."

"Yes." Mr. Kitaro's eyes soften. "She was my great-aunt. Older sister to my grandmother."

The hint of a smile materialized in Darshana's expression. "Yes, I had the pleasure of meeting her—and working with her when she lived at the palace. Seems like ages ago."

"It's been over twenty years since she passed."

A shadow fell over Darshana's face, and her gaze seemed far away.

"We have the dagger he's been guarding," Jae told her.

This seemed to bring Darshana out of her daze. She clasped her hands together and faced the Sacred Key.

"Mr. Kitaro, what do you know of the dark mages?"

"I've heard some theories, but I can't be sure if any of them are correct. The detailed existence of dark mages seems to have been kept from the Sacred Keys. Or at least attempted to be kept from them."

She kept her eyes on him, scrutinizing his face as if trying to determine if he was covering up something.

"You don't believe me," he said. When she smirked in response, he let out a small chuckle. "Okay. Why don't you tell us *your* theory, and I'll let you know if any of it matches with the rumors I've heard."

Darshana looked around the room. "Perhaps we should move to the living room and give young Huojin some peace and quiet."

Five

Salina and Mayhara sat on the living room couch. Shiro stood at the back of the room, one arm wrapped around himself and the other propped up as he stroked his chin. Jae settled on the arm of the couch, his hands pressed into his legs right above his knees. Darshana paced the room as she spoke, while Mr. Kitaro stood and listened with his hands clasped in front of him.

"Kashmeru has sent his shadow army to capture the Lotus. We know this to be true. We've all witnessed this manifestation firsthand. The legend says the Council of the Seven needs Lakshmi's blood to unlock Kashmeru's tomb. The Council of the Seven has always been described as dark mages, but the elders and gurus of the empire have always counted on the notion that the Seven were elite Pishacha soldiers—spirits as ancient as Kashmeru who have been at his side through the centuries. But seeing the dark mage who attacked us on the bridge, I'm leaning toward the theory that they are not Pishacha. That they are people born as mages, just like you." Darshana gestured to the mages and then folded her hands together as she continued to pace.

"The ones we saw in the cave looked around our age," Salina said. "But they weren't from the academy."

"I'm not sure of their background," Darshana said. "Or why their existence has been kept secret."

"Probably for the same reason the reincarnation of the Lotus has been kept secret," Mr. Kitaro said. "To have an upper hand in this war."

"So they've been training to fight for Kashmeru?" Shiro asked. "Training with whom? And where?"

Darshana shook her head. "More mysteries I don't have the answers to."

"Kashmeru must have created them," Jae said.

"It makes sense that they're working with the government." Mayhara raked her fingers through her hair. "Mages are illegal. Yet these mages walk free."

Darshana eyed the Sacred Key. "How does my theory stand against what you've heard, Mr. Kitaro?"

Mr. Kitaro's gaze roamed about the room. He took his time before he spoke, as if measuring his words. "Most of the rumors circling the elders of the empire have been of the existence of mage children who were not brought forward. It didn't make sense at first because we do not force anyone to swear themselves to the Lotus if it is not their will. Most mages, of course, feel honored to be a part of such an important society, to be invited to the mage academy—when it existed—to train. And those families who declined the invitation were few but documented in the Sacred books. We respected their wishes. Therefore, it had become curious that rumors surfaced of hidden mages, families who hid their children from existence."

"These families must have been seduced by

Kashmeru." Darshana wrung her hands. "Kashmeru could have sensed the presence of dark mage powers and… I don't know. Promised them something great for their loyalty, perhaps."

Mr. Kitaro nodded. "Most likely an agreement to spare them from the downfall of the universe. A place in his kingdom when the rest of humanity would be erased."

"And now they've come out of hiding and are leading the fight." Salina's voice was barely audible.

"The Council of the Seven." Mayhara looked at Jae. "There are seven of them."

"And there are seven elite to match their power," Jae said. "We just need to find them."

"But they won't be able to fulfill the prophecy without the daggers, right?" Shiro asked. "They play a part."

Salina stood. "Then we need to get the rest of the daggers. Before they do."

Six

Jae found Mr. Kitaro standing alone in the middle of the downstairs hall, staring at one of the stone statues. The older man held a coffee mug in his hands, his expression grim.

"Mr. Kitaro?"

He seemed to snap out of his trance and turned toward Jae. "Oh, I'm sorry. Did you need me for something?"

"Um, no." Jae stepped closer. "Is everything all right?"

Mr. Kitaro let out a long sigh. "To be honest, I was thinking about Aiguo."

"Your bodyguard." Jae furrowed his brow "Did you hear from him?"

"Not since he diverted the Pishacha from following us, no. And if I'm telling the truth, I'm not too optimistic about ever seeing or hearing from him again."

"You… You think they killed him."

"I hate to admit it. I don't want to simply give up hope, but it's not looking good." Mr. Kitaro gazed down at his coffee. "He saved our lives. He was a good man. He was loyal, did his job, and he has brought honor onto himself."

"I'm sorry for your loss," Jae said quietly. He drew closer to the Sacred Key and placed a hand on his shoulder. "We will beat the Pishacha, Mr. Kitaro. Whatever it takes. We won't let Aiguo's sacrifice be in vain.

☙

The air was stifling. Salina swiped a hand over her throat and walked toward the rear sliding doors that led to the patio. She needed some air. As soon as she slid the door open, a cool wind caressed her skin. The mountain air was slightly damp, but Salina didn't mind. It refreshed her. It nourished her need to escape for a moment.

Sitting on the ground by the koi pond was Shiro. He stared at his fingers as he braided two blades of grass together. Taking slow strides, Salina concentrated on easy, deliberate breaths as she headed for the white, wooden bench Shiro was sitting in front of.

For a moment, they simply sat there. Together but separate.

Shiro tossed his braided-grass creation into the pond. A copper glow emanated from his palm as he waved his hand to the side. The water in the pond responded to his powers by rippling toward the floating grass braid, pushing it along the surface of the water.

One of the koi in the path of the ripple changed direction and quickly swam away from the charging braid. Shiro twisted his wrist, and the braid chased after the fish.

After a minute of watching his shenanigans, Salina

couldn't help but let out a laugh. Shiro glanced over his shoulder at her. The corners of his mouth inched upward.

"I'm glad to see you actually have a smile." Shiro shifted to face her. "I was beginning to think one didn't exist in your culture."

Salina raised a brow. "I could say the same about you."

He ducked his head and chuckled.

Salina raised her chin as her gaze went to the sky. The faint, streaky haze of the Akutake comet stared back at her, as if encouraging her to stay strong for their mission. She breathed in a shuddered breath, hoping Huojin would heal and be able to fight their fight.

"That about sums it up," Shiro said. "That sigh. It's made of a million words and a billion emotions."

She nodded, but her eyes were still fixed on the comet. "It's been hard. I don't know if you remember, but back at the academy, I was notorious for being a positive person. I was always able to find the good in any situation. But after my mom passed… and now, not knowing Huojin's fate… I don't know if I even have it in me to stay positive."

When she turned toward him, she found he'd been

studying her face.

"You really care about her," he said.

"Yes, of course."

He continued to stare at her, and she found the intensity unnerving.

A light coming to life inside the temple caught Salina's attention. She spotted Jae through the glass doors aiming a remote control at the televiewer. The news popped up on the screen, and Jae and Mayhara watched with concentration as they sat together on the couch. Salina couldn't hear the televiewer, but the newscaster on the screen reminded Salina of all the times Huojin would watch the news for word on the prison camps. It suddenly hit her that Huojin had spent years worried about the wellbeing of her parents, and now it was Huojin who was in critical condition, and her parents had no idea.

She turned to face Shiro. He wasn't staring at her anymore.

"What was it like in the prison camps?" she asked.

Shiro's eyes widened for a second, obviously surprised by her question.

"I see what you mean about always focusing on the positive," he joked.

"I'm sorry. I was just… wondering about Huojin's family."

"Ah. Okay." He ripped another two blades of grass from the ground and began folding them together. "It was awful, if I can be honest. It was like being stripped of your humanity and not knowing what terrors the next day might bring."

"I'm sorry you had to go through that."

"It got a little easier when Qiang took me under his wing. He not only gave me tips on how to survive, he gave me a reason to survive."

"Yeah." She gave him a half-smile. "Huojin did the same with me."

"It made all the difference in the world. I grew to love him, to the point that I knew I could only exist if Qiang was in my life. That without his love, I could perish." He finished folding his blades of grass and looked up at her. "Is that how you feel about Huojin?"

Her smile was soft. "No. I mean, I love her, but not like that. She's my best friend. Not that I think there's anything wrong with your love for Qiang."

He averted his eyes.

"Did I say something wrong?" She placed a hand on

her heart. "I'm sorry if I offended you."

"No. It's not that." He threw the blades of grass to the side and pushed himself to his feet. Shoving his hands in his pockets, he shrugged. "I've come to realize that I don't know if Qiang feels the same way for me. There was a split-second moment during our escape where we got separated. And it seemed all too easy for him to let me go."

"But you can't really judge his feelings from a moment of panic."

Shiro shrugged again, kicking at the dirt. "I've been looking online, searching for any prisoner deaths, just in case. But I can't find any news. So if he's dead, they're keeping it a secret. And if he's alive, why hasn't he tried to contact me?"

"Shiro, it's not exactly easy to find us here."

Shiro shook his head. "He would find a way. His ingenuity is one thing I admired about him."

Salina pursed her lips. Her attention was drawn back to the televiewer. On the screen was an image of a building ablaze with fire. Curious, she stood and headed inside. Shiro followed.

Video footage on the screen showed fire fighters

battling a burning building.

"—the police station is a mere one hundred kilometers from New Jaipur. Damages are extensive. The fire claimed the lives of six Imperial Police officers and left another four with critical burns. Authorities have not yet had a chance to investigate the source of the explosion, but word is an extremist group is suspect in the attack."

"An explosion?" Salina asked, crossing her arms.

"Do you think it was really an extremist group?" Mayhara asked. "Or could it be the Pishacha? Or the dark mages?"

Shiro worried at his chin, shaking his head.

"They're working together," Jae said. "Why would they attack the ones working with them?"

"Maybe they messed up." Salina shrugged. "Did something they weren't supposed to do."

The image on the screen changed first to a close-up shot of the Akutake comet and then changed to a number of people dressed in suits and a handful of uniformed Imperial Police entering the town hall.

"—to discuss the events welcoming the Akutake comet. Due to the alleged extremists' attack on the Alwar police station, the chief of New Jaipur's Imperial Police is scheduled to accompany the governor, along with an advisory committee. Governor Laghari will lead the opening ceremony of the Navratri Festival, giving what is sure to be a spiritual speech for the citizens of, not only New Jaipur, but all of New United Asia. The nine nights of the Navratri Festival will be filled with music and performances, with traditional—"

Mayhara stood from the couch. "That woman who was standing beside the chief of police. That was my boss back at the census bureau."

"And the officer next to him," Jae added. "He's the guy from a picture Mayhara and I saw at Bruno's club.

"He was at the office, too." Mayhara tapped her chin with a finger. "He had a meeting with my boss. They're all connected with the Pishacha."

"Your boss is the one who had the scrolls, right?" Salina asked.

"Yes." Mayhara began to pace.

"Are you thinking what I'm thinking?" Jae asked her.

"We should go to the festival?" Mayhara bit her lip.

"What?" Shiro scoffed. "We can't just show up, an escapee and a wanted murderer, to a place crawling with Imperial Police."

"They must have information on the whereabouts of the first dagger," Jae said. "We could follow them or listen in on their conversations. It could be a long shot, but we've got to do what we can to get that dagger."

"It's risky," Salina said.

Jae got up from the couch and stood beside Mayhara. "So is doing nothing."

"We'll need to keep out of sight." Shiro rubbed at his chin. "But you're right. One of them could lead us to the dagger."

"Long shots are still shots." The voice was Darshana's.

They turned to see her standing in the doorway. She had a thick shawl wrapped around her shoulders.

"Darshana, where are you going?" Jae asked. "Shouldn't you be resting?"

"I've rested long enough." She shuffled a set of keys between her hands. "I'm going back to the swamp to see if Amalia can help Huojin."

"Alone?" Mayhara asked.

"Mr. Kitaro has agreed to watch over Huojin, and the rest of you have work to do. The rest of the daggers are out there, as well as Sacred Keys whose lives are at stake. And we're still shy a few elite mages." She nodded once to them before she turned on her heel and left the room.

"She's right," Jae said. "Let's get moving."

"I'll get the scroll. We can start there." Mayhara turned to Shiro. "And I'm close to getting an exact location on one of the elite. I'll narrow down an address so you can follow that lead."

Shiro nodded. "Let's do it."

Seven

Naree gazed out the car window as the dark mage put the vehicle in PARK. She'd been twisting the same strands of hair between her fingers during the long drive, fighting off the feeling of being on edge. Anytime she felt the panic inside her coming to the surface, she could hear Kashmeru's voice telling her everything was evolving as it was supposed to. That they'd be together soon.

One of the dark mages who had accompanied her opened her car door and stepped aside. Naree climbed out, still staring at the view before them.

"It's been a long time since I've seen the shore," she said, her voice calm.

"Yes, Your Highness." The mage motioned for her to walk in front of him. "We can enjoy the view later. First we must get this dagger."

With a sigh, she turned away from the sea and led the way.

Eight

Mayhara checked the scroll again, the wind blowing over the nearby sea causing her hair to whip around her head. She could feel Jae's body heat as he drew near. His breath was warm on her neck, but she knew his eyes were on the map.

"This must be it," she said, more to convince herself than anyone else.

There was nothing around for miles except a tall, red-

and-white lighthouse. They'd traveled over fifteen hours to Jamnagar, following suspicious activity on the scroll, only to come to a lonely and seemingly abandoned but functioning lighthouse on the coast. Jae and Mayhara had decided to chase the lead, while Salina and Shiro traveled to New Delhi to track down the amethyst mage.

Waves crashed upon the shore, and a brutal wind bit into Mayhara's skin. She wasn't used to the chill in the air, and she felt the need to close the distance between herself and Jae, seeking out his warmth for comfort.

"The two black triangles that were flashing on the map have disappeared." Mayhara looked up at the top of the lighthouse. "It's got to be the dark mages. Do you think they disappear if they're inside a building?"

"I wouldn't rule it out. Let's go in and find out."

He nodded to her, a silent message for her to be prepared. If a dark mage—or two—was inside the building, they were going to be ready for a fight.

Seagulls squawked through the foggy air. Mayhara's fingers twitched as she and Jae stomped over rocks and wet sand. They had one dagger, and the Pishacha had one. If one of the daggers was still here, she would feel like they might be okay. Like they stood a chance in this fight. But if there was no dagger here, if the Pishacha had gotten to it first…

The pathway in front of the lighthouse was cracked and broken, demolished beyond repair, the earth beneath it uneven and full of sunken-in gaps. Mayhara opened her fingers, her palms still aimed at the ground. The red glow of her garnet wristband matched the red in her palms. She pushed out her power, reaching for the earth below them. The ground shook as the dirt below the broken path evened out, the gaps disappearing. She and Jae picked up their pace to get to the lighthouse door.

Taking a chance, she turned the knob. The door was unlocked. She gave Jae a nod before pushing it open and stepping inside.

They paused in the entryway in front of the spiral stairway that led up the tower. Jae held a finger up, his neck stretching upward. His palms glowed a bright blue.

"It's quiet," he said. "I don't think anyone is here."

"Who'd hide a dagger in a lighthouse?" she whispered.

"Who'd think to *look* for one in a lighthouse? Let's go up and see if we can find anything."

Their footfalls sounded on the metal steps. Jae

quickly used his powers to silence them. Mayhara felt as if every nerve in her body was on high alert as they climbed. It felt as if they'd never reach the top, but at long last, the bright blaze of the turning beacon came into view.

Mayhara held tightly to the railing at the top of the stairs. The windows around them were enormous, the view stunning. But the lighthouse was empty.

"Did we make a mistake?" Mayhara asked. "Was the map wrong?"

"Maybe they took the dagger *and* the Sacred Key."

"There are no signs of a struggle." Mayhara shook her head. "I don't know. Something's not right."

"Maybe a Key hid the dagger here but didn't stick around to guard it."

"Doesn't sound like something a Sacred Key would do."

"I know. Let's head down and see if we can find any clues."

When they reached the bottom of the stairs, Mayhara put a hand on the wall, following it around.

"There's a door back here," she said.

"I think that's the control room." Jae pressed an ear

to the door. "I can hear the motor for the beacon, but nothing else."

Mayhara turned the door handle and slowly pushed the door open. When she switched on the light inside the room, she and Jae gasped.

In the middle of the room was a wooden chair. A man was tied to the chair, his head slacking to the side and his eyes rolled back. A trickle of dried blood stained his face from the corner of his mouth to his chin.

"You think he was a Key?" Mayhara asked.

"Why else would he have been killed?"

Mayhara forced herself to look away from the corpse and focus on the other objects in the room. A desk was overturned, its drawers ripped from their places and tossed on the floor. A short bookshelf sat empty. Folders, papers, and books were strewn about, and a cabinet stood with its doors wide open, its contents obviously rifled through. A nail stuck out of one wall, the picture frame that must have been hanging there broken on the floor. "If there was a dagger hidden here, chances are they found it. All the shelves and drawers appear to have been searched already."

Jae scrubbed a hand down his face and nodded.

"Okay. But maybe they didn't find it. We need to be sure. Let's feel around. Maybe there's a loose brick in the wall or something, a hidden spot they might not have found."

After searching for a few minutes, Mayhara backed away from the wall, almost tripping on the small rug that sat underneath the wooden chair. An idea hit her when she looked down at it. Crouching down, she placed her hands on the floor and reached out with her mage powers. She could feel a lack of earth below her, a place not occupied by the ground.

"There's something under the floor. A room, I think." She looked up at Jae, her mouth set in a straight line. "We have to move the body to get underneath."

Jae took a deep breath and nodded. "Okay. We'll set him on the floor off to the side. Let's untie him."

"Be gentle." Mayhara knew it was a useless request. The man was already dead. Still, she couldn't help but feel they needed to treat the Sacred Key with respect.

After they undid the ropes, Jae and Mayhara lifted the man's slumped form out of the chair. He was heavy, but Mayhara did her best not to drop him. Still, the man's bald head thumped on the floor once they set him down. Mayhara grimaced and whispered an apology to the dead man.

Jae picked up the chair and moved it aside. Mayhara rolled back the rug. She didn't see any difference in the floorboards, but she felt around to be sure. On one end of a board, there was a tiny notch just big enough for a finger to fit.

"A trapdoor," she said.

She stuck her finger in the notch and pulled. There was a creaky groan as she lifted the door. Using his Linq, Jae lit up the area to look into the hole in the floor.

"Another staircase," he said. "I'll go down first."

Jae disappeared down the stairs. As Mayhara began to climb in after him, she heard a click, and the space lit up fully. They found themselves in an underground room. There were cabinets and a desk. A small military-style bed was pushed up against the wall. It was like an underground bunker.

Mayhara wrinkled her brow. "Nothing looks out of place. I don't think whoever killed the man knew this room was here."

"Then we might be in luck."

The two of them wasted no time searching the room. They opened all the drawers, felt for false bottoms, and reached behind the furniture for where a box might have been securely taped. Reaching for an oversized book on the bookshelf, Mayhara pulled, only the hardback cover slipped away, revealing a black box standing on its side.

"Jae."

He came over as she took the box off the shelf. It was decorated in a shiny red-and-gold pattern. Mayhara held her breath as she turned it right-side-up and opened it.

Inside, lying neatly in a velvet mold, was a silver dagger. It had the same intricate design and grooves as the one they'd taken from Naree.

"They never found it," she said. "The Sacred Key did his job. He protected it."

She and Jae exchanged glances.

"We've got to get it back to the temple. The Pishacha might come back."

Securing the black box in his canvas bag, Jae led the way back up the stairs. Mayhara replaced the rug, and Jae set the chair on top of it.

"What about him?" she asked, her eyes on the Sacred Key.

Jae let out a shuddered breath. "I'm afraid we can't do anything. I can call in an anonymous tip to the

Imperial Police, though they might already know about this if they're working with the Pishacha."

"Won't they trace the call?"

"No, I have a program that hides that information. Don't worry."

Mayhara bent down to close the Key's eyes. "No. Don't call them. They won't treat him with any respect. I have a better idea. Will you help me carry him outside?"

He did as she requested, the two of them lugging the honorable man outside of the lighthouse.

"Over here." Mayhara gestured with her chin.

After they set him down on the ground, Mayhara closed her eyes. She recited a prayer in her head, thanking the gods for the Sacred Key, giving thanks for his help. Then she held her hands out, focusing on the ground around him. As her palms glowed a bright red, the earth shook, the dirt and sand around the man falling away. It was as if the earth was enveloping the Sacred Key in its arms, pulling him in and forming a shelter around him. As his form disappeared into the earth, Mayhara waved her arms over the ground, and the earth evened out. No one would be able to tell anyone was buried there.

"May he have peace," she said.

Jae put a gentle hand on her shoulder. "That was nice of you."

"He didn't deserve to be left there for the flies."

Jae nodded, not saying a word.

Together, they turned away from the makeshift grave and headed for Jae's bike.

Nine

Mayhara sat across from Director Shei, her hands folded in her lap. Glancing over at one of the large windows in her office, she caught a glimpse at her reflection. She swiped a strand of hair behind her ear. There was something different about the way she looked. This was not how she looked now. This look was from her past. From when she was younger.

"I have to admit I'm impressed with what I've read."

Director Shei's voice caused Mayhara to turn away from her reflection.

She swallowed hard and forced a small smile. "Thank you."

"Your records show you excel at administrative work. I think you'll be a great asset to the team." Director Shei's brown eyes flit over Mayhara's face. "Do you understand the responsibilities we're about to place in your hands?"

"Yes, of course."

Director Shei set her elbows on the desk and pressed her smooth hands together, her beautifully polished nails clicking together as she did so. "Your family will be kept safe. We promise you that, in exchange for your services to the firm. I know how important family is."

Mayhara followed Shei's gaze to the picture frame standing on the corner of her desk. In the photograph, Director Shei stood beside a girl about Mayhara's age. She had straight, black hair and thick streaks of eyeliner. The young girl was not smiling and looked as if she were about to turn away from the camera.

"Is that your daughter?" Mayhara asked.

"Yes. That's my Ruolan. I call her 'Ru.'"

Mayhara reached for the picture frame, but her hands

were unsteady. The frame fell, and when Mayhara reached for it, Jae's hand suddenly appeared to pick it up.

"We need to hurry," Jae said.

Mayhara looked around to find herself in the dark. Jae placed a piece of sheer, plastic material on Director Shei's mouse and pressed it against one of the drawers of her desk. The drawer opened.

It was the night they'd broken into her old office building.

Mayhara gasped, sitting upright in bed. Two memories had converged in her dream, and each of them was connected to an important piece of the puzzle.

She threw her sheets off and grabbed her robe, barely fitting her feet into her slippers before she charged out of her room and down the stairs. She ran past the office, but no one was in there. The lit-up monitor told her Jae must have been awake, so she quickly changed direction and darted for the kitchen.

"Jae," she called.

When she skidded into the kitchen, Jae stood with a cup of coffee. Darshana was in front of him. They both turned to her, concern on their faces.

"Darshana, Jae." She put a hand on her chest, begging

her heart to stop trying to slam through her chest.

"Slow down, child," Darshana told her.

"What's wrong?" Jae asked. "Did something happen?"

"The girl. The female dark mage from the cave, the one who followed me through the street fair—"

"Yeah?" He narrowed his eyes, waiting for her to continue.

"She's director Shei's daughter."

Jae blinked, shaking his head. Darshana closed her eyes and placed her fingertips together, resting them on her chin.

"How do you know this?" Jae asked.

"I know it sounds crazy, but it came to me in a dream. Something my mind remembered from the director's office."

Jae put his coffee cup down. "What was it?"

"There was a picture on her desk. Do you remember when we broke in? I knocked it down."

"I… vaguely remember?"

"There was a girl in the picture with the director. That girl is the same one I saw at the food fair when I went to get Huojin. She's the dark mage we fought in

Naree's cave. And in my dream, I remembered when I was first being interviewed for the company. Director Shei told me it was her daughter. I'd just forgotten about it."

"That explains why she's connected," Jae said. "She plays a bigger part in this than we thought."

"We'll have to tell the others," Darshana said. "It makes me wonder about the other dark mages. Perhaps there are more people in power because of their dark mage offspring. Jae, would you mind having everyone gather in the meditation room?"

"Yes. Right away." Jae bowed and left the kitchen.

"It's probably not the breakthrough we were looking for," Mayhara said to Darshana, "but it's something. Especially after Shiro and Salina came to a dead end searching for the other elites."

"It could very well help."

Mayhara had some hope in her heart. Her information on the last known residences of the other elites had turned out to be nothing but abandoned apartments. The only documented elite mage in a prison camp was the emerald mage. Mayhara doubted any of the mages knew they were now elite. And one of them was currently in a prison camp.

When they were all gathered in the meditation room, Mayhara was surprised to see Huojin. Salina had to help her walk, but her healing process seemed to have accelerated. The salve Darshana had fetched from the swamp witch was working wonders.

Salina helped Huojin sit on a yoga pillow and then took a seat herself.

"I thought this would be a good opportunity to catch up on where we are." Darshana sat cross-legged facing them. "The comet is getting closer, and the festival will begin in a couple days. Huojin is healing, and Mayhara has just informed me that one of the dark mages is the daughter of the census bureau's director. We have two daggers, and the Pishacha—as far as we know—have one. Jae has told me that the scroll makers have not yet gotten back to him with information on the cryptic scroll we have."

"I'll pay them another visit," Jae said. "They may be avoiding me because of the Pishacha."

Darshana nodded. "Then be careful. They might be watching the shop."

"I've been tracking the black triangles on the other

scroll. But so far, I've come up empty," Shiro said. "I'm beginning to believe the Pishacha aren't able to locate the other daggers, either."

"All this aside," Darshana said, "I want you to remember that we will inevitably be fighting the big fight. You will have to call upon your training from the academy as well as learn some lessons you never had a chance to learn because the school closed down."

Mayhara took a deep breath.

"What if we can't learn in time?" Huojin looked down at her bandages.

Darshana kept her chin up. "The elite mages are destined to go into battle no matter what you have learned and what you haven't."

"We don't have all the elite mages yet," Salina said. "And some of us are not in the best shape."

Darshana waved a hand in the air. "Mind over matter. Do not dwell on the problem. Focus your mind on the solution. You have to believe the universe will deliver the answers. The other elite mages will be found, and your powers will excel as they should to protect the world from Kashmeru's destruction."

Huojin ducked her head. Salina grabbed her hand

and squeezed it.

"But first," Darshana said, "we must meditate."

The following days were a whirlwind of activity. Jae returned to the scroll shop to put pressure on the scroll maker family, but he still had no answers. The other elite mages were nowhere to be found. The locations of the remaining daggers also remained a mystery. When the mages weren't running around trying to get a leg up in the war, Darshana made them train.

While Mayhara literally made mountains out of molehills, Jae irritated Shiro by practicing his truth power on him. Huojin started back slowly, but in a matter of days, she was able to practice with the rest of them. She was still weak, but Salina encouraged her, telling her she was getting stronger every day.

Darshana now told her it was time to push herself, so they all went into the field behind the temple for a mock battle of ice and fire. Shiro against Huojin.

Huojin looked to Salina, who gave her a confident

nod.

Taking their stances across from each other, Shiro and Huojin held their hands up.

"Remember, Huojin," Darshana called out, "control your breathing. Inhale through the nose and exhale through the mouth."

Shiro, who seemed to be waiting for Huojin to stop breathing so heavily, flipped his wrist and shot out a blast of ice. Huojin grunted as she threw a fireball to deflect it. The fireball nicked the ice but didn't quite repel it. It zoomed close to Huojin, who had to dive to the side to avoid it.

"Your flame needs to be more contained to give it strength," Darshana said.

Huojin huffed out an agitated breath and took her stance again. This time she shot fire at Shiro first. With a wave of his hand, a shield of ice formed, virtually swallowing Huojin's fireball.

"The heat needs to flow through you effortlessly," Darshana instructed. "Like the breath of a dragon."

Huojin squared her jaw and shook out her hands.

"You can do it, Huojin!" Salina called out.

Huojin assumed the position, her breaths deliberate.

Shiro nodded to her, as if giving her a heads-up. He crouched low and threw his hands out. Ice bullets shot from his palms.

Huojin shouted as she placed both hands in front of her and created a wall of fire. The fire wall deflected most of the ice, but one ice bullet got through and hit her in the arm. Huojin spun as she was knocked backward, falling to her knees as she grabbed the spot that had been struck.

"Your emotions are fueling your fire, but you do not have them under control." Darshana linked her hands in front of her. "You need to harness your anger and your frustrations without letting them burn the power out of your flames."

"I'm trying," Huojin said, her voice cracking. "I can't do it."

"This isn't up for debate. You *must* do it."

"Darshana," Salina began, but the guru cut her off.

"I'm sorry, but there is no room for being lenient. Every elite has to do their part. The universe is counting on you. And you owe it to the Lotus to fight this battle."

Tears flowed down Huojin's face. She shook her head and stormed off, heading inside the temple. Salina ran after her.

Mayhara exchanged looks with Jae, not sure what to do. She'd never seen Darshana like this.

"Darshana." Mayhara's voice was gentle as she approached her. "Are you okay?"

Darshana closed her eyes and rubbed at her temples. When she opened her eyes again, she let out a long breath. "Please forgive me. I lost control and forgot my mindfulness. I believe I need to take a silent walk and reflect on my actions."

"Yes, of course."

The guru bowed to the remaining mages and walked past the koi pond and into the trees.

Jae, Mayhara, and Shiro stood in silence, not knowing what to say. The stress was getting to them. To all of them. Mayhara raked a hand through her hair, wondering if they had what it took to win this battle or if everything was going to fall apart.

Ten

Naree approached the young man and smiled. He looked up from his desk and tilted his head.

"May I help you?" he asked.

She studied his face for a moment, and then her palms glowed blue. "You're the sapphire elite," she said.

"Yes." He narrowed his eyes at first, noticing her palms.

Naree smiled. He could not lie; she'd used truth powers on him. He had a blocker chip in his neck, so he couldn't stop her without causing himself pain.

Then, the Pishacha and dark mages entered the office behind Naree, and the young man's eyes widened. He tripped as he shot up from his chair, his hands held out to regain his balance.

"W-What's going on here?" He visibly swallowed. "How'd you get in here?"

"Shhhhh." Naree playfully held a finger to her lips. "You're not going to scream, are you?"

His gaze whipped quickly between the men behind her. His jaw quivered as he shook his head. "N-No."

"Hmm. Cross your heart?" Naree stepped even closer, her palms raised to face him. "Hope to die?"

Eleven

Huojin turned away from the mirror. It wasn't just that her burns looked awful, but she couldn't seem to face her reflection at all. There was no fire behind her eyes anymore. She felt lost. Disappointment from the last three days of training weighed heavily on her heart to the point of proving unbearable.

Darshana's outburst during the first training at the

temple still echoed in her head. Since then, Darshana's words had been strictly helpful criticism, absent of the harsh tone she'd used with Huojin that day. Apparently, the guru had done some mindfulness meditation and cleared the cruelty from her instructions. But Huojin still felt Darshana's dissatisfaction with every word.

There was a knock on her door, which had been left slightly ajar. When Huojin spotted Salina peeking into her room, she smiled at her and waved her in.

"You coming to dinner?" Salina stepped into the room wearing a simple yellow dress, but the way it looked on her was like runway fashion on a supermodel.

"Yeah." Huojin felt as if Salina could tell her smile was fake. "Let's go."

Salina didn't question her façade. Instead, she hooked her arm through Huojin's and walked beside her as they headed toward the dining room.

As they descended the marble staircase, Huojin's stomach began to churn, and not from hunger. Though she had faced Darshana every day, it never got easier. In fact, she could swear that the stress of not believing she could fulfill her destiny was eating a hole in her heart.

The dining room was more like a banquet hall. The

gray and white ceramic table was big enough to seat twenty. The tabletop reflected the warm lights of the lotus-shaped chandelier above it. Darshana, Jae, and Mayhara were already seated and looked up at Huojin and Salina as they entered. Huojin's gaze immediately dropped to the floor when she and Darshana caught each other's eyes. She followed Salina's lead as they slipped into their chairs.

"Smells delicious," Salina said.

Shiro emerged from the adjoined kitchen carrying a large serving bowl of steaming rice, which he set upon the table between a plate of yakitori chicken and *goma-ae*. A waft of herbs and spices filled the air.

"The chicken is a little spicy," Shiro said. "I hope everyone is okay with that."

"The spicier the better," Salina said.

"I think I can handle it." Jae grabbed his cloth napkin and spread it out on his lap.

"Looks divine," Darshana told Shiro as he sat down to join them.

Mr. Kitaro appeared at the entrance in a nice button-up shirt. "I hope I'm not too late."

"Not at all, Mr. Kitaro," Shiro said, gesturing for him

to take one of the empty seats.

"This was a lovely idea, Shiro." Darshana nodded at him. "Thank you for going through all the trouble."

"My pleasure," Shiro replied. "I felt like everyone's been working so hard, we deserve a small reward. Something to keep the spirit alive and full of thanks."

Huojin simply stared as the rest of the group began placing food on their plates. She had no appetite. The feeling of failure filled every inch of her, not leaving room for anything else. She looked around, studying the faces of her fellow mages, her guru, and the Sacred Key. This dinner was for them. Not her. She hadn't done anything to deserve it.

As the conversation gradually transitioned from how delicious the food was into their theories on the Pishacha's strategies, Huojin could do nothing but set her hands in her lap and force back the lump in her throat. Except for being shunned as a mage, she'd never felt like an outsider before. But during the past few days, she'd felt more and more like she didn't belong. Like some higher power had made a mistake in including her with the mage community. Like she was an imposter.

Salina leaned closer to her. "You okay?" she

whispered.

Huojin looked up at her, wanting to reveal everything she was feeling, but she couldn't do it here in front of everyone.

Salina's eyes suddenly widened. "Oh, you're bleeding."

Everyone stopped talking and focused on Huojin. She followed Salina's gaze to her leg, where a blossom of blood had begun to spread through the leg of her trousers. She hadn't realized she had been digging her fingers into her thigh, breaking open one of her wounds.

"Let's change your bandage before the blood dries." Salina stood. "Hopefully the bandage hasn't slipped like last time. We don't want cloth stuck to your skin."

When Salina held out a hand to her, Huojin took it and stood, not even acknowledging the pain of her open wound. She nodded to the rest of the group.

"I'm so sorry. Please continue your meal without me."

"It's no problem at all, Huojin." Mayhara set down her fork. "Do you need any help?"

"It's okay," Salina said. "We've got this. But thanks."

Huojin walked ahead of Salina, her arms wrapped

around her midsection. She was so nauseous, she couldn't even look behind her to see if Salina was still there. It wasn't until she reached her room that she knew Salina was still with her.

"Sit down." Salina motioned toward the bed. "I'll get the bandages."

Huojin wiped at her cheek, catching a tear. She grinded her teeth, frustrated that she felt trapped in a place where nobody wanted her.

"Actually," Salina said as she studied her, "you're going to have to get out of those pants."

Huojin sniffed back more tears as she nodded, standing and unbuttoning her pants. She slipped them off and tossed them toward the wastebasket near her door. "They're ruined anyway."

Salina looked as if she wanted to say something to that, but the tightening of her lips told Huojin that Salina had changed her mind. Perhaps it was one of Salina's family recipes on how to get blood out of clothes. Normally, she would have been glad to hear Salina's advice. Normally, they would conquer such a project together, no doubt falling into a fit of hysterics over their clumsiness.

But not tonight. Tonight, more than anything, Huojin wanted to escape.

She sat far enough over the edge of the bed that Salina could unwrap her bloodied bandages. She winced at the burn of the cloth being torn from her wound but bit her tongue to keep from making any remarks.

"Sorry," Salina said. "I'll be quick. Looks like you punctured it. Probably with your nails. Why were you squeezing your leg so hard?"

Huojin looked into Salina's eyes, unwilling to tell her the truth about how she was feeling. "It was itching. I didn't realize I'd scratched at it so hard."

"It's okay." Salina gave her a half-shrug as she unrolled a fresh spool of gauze. "It happens. Do you remember when I scraped up my hand when I first started training at the academy? I couldn't stop scratching at it. Had to wear a glove to class just to keep me from messing with it."

Huojin offered her the smallest of smiles, but there wasn't enough feeling behind it. It was as if the disappointment she felt in herself kept her from enjoying anything, even the smallest of things.

"Okay." Salina stood and looked at her own hands,

which were spotted with blood. "You can get dressed. I'm going to wash up."

"You should go back to dinner," Huojin told her. "Shiro went through all the trouble to cook."

"What about you?"

"I'm not actually feeling so well." She rubbed a hand across her belly. "I don't want to make it worse by introducing hot spices to the mix. But please tell Shiro I'm sorry."

"He'll understand. Don't worry." Salina picked up a stray piece of gauze from the floor and tossed it in the trash. "You going to rest, then?"

"Yeah, I'm going to lie down for a bit."

"I'll come back later. Do you need anything?"

"No need to come back. I'm probably going to sleep." Again, Huojin forced a small smile. "Enjoy your evening. I'll see you in the morning."

Salina came forward, holding her blood-stained hands out to her side, and hugged Huojin with her forearms. "I need to go wash up. Goodnight."

After Salina left, Huojin closed her door. Pressing her head against the wood, she swallowed the lump in her throat and sniffed back the tears that began to flow. She was suffering, both physically and mentally. She wasn't sure how she was going to get through this.

Twelve

Huojin could hear the mumble of conversation and trickles of laughter from downstairs. She turned in her bed, her eyes catching the illuminated digits of the clock on her nightstand. The group had to be done with their dinner by now, but it appeared the evening of camaraderie wasn't over. Huojin thought her dose of pain medication would have helped her to fall into a deep sleep; however, it seemed to have the opposite effect tonight. Though she longed to drift away, it simply wasn't happening.

Throwing her covers off her body, Huojin slipped her legs over the side of the bed and sat up, staring at her balcony doors. Maybe some fresh air would do the trick. Darshana always said that the surroundings of nature helped, and there was no better view of the mountaintop woods than from the second floor of the temple.

A soft wind swirled around her as she opened the balcony doors and stepped outside. The tender chirp of crickets welcomed her, and the stars twinkled above her. Her eyes went to the white streak of the comet only momentarily before she tore her gaze away from it and looked down at the koi pond in the rear gardens. She didn't need another reminder of how she was failing to fulfill her duty.

The distant sound of a car horn caught her attention. If she leaned out enough and turned to the right, she could just make out the road that traversed the mountain. She watched a few cars drive by, imagining the people below going about their everyday lives, free to go wherever they wanted without the responsibility she had on her shoulders. Why were they so lucky to be free? Why did this major accountability have to be her destiny?

Her hope was gone. There was no way she could do this. Someone or something out there had made a mistake in picking her to carry out this task. It would be better if she left.

Tears ran down her cheeks. She never thought she could be this disloyal to the Lotus empress. She'd devoted her whole life to her, yet now, she didn't believe she had anything left in her to offer the empress. Nothing but failure.

Turning swiftly on her heel, she charged back into her room and grabbed her duffle bag from the closet. She couldn't stay here anymore. She had nothing to contribute to the cause. She would only be a burden to the group, and she'd lost the skills to be able to fight the Pishacha anyway. She had to leave.

She threw her things into the duffle bag and slipped on dark pants and her forest green sweatshirt. She quickly grabbed some supplies to change her bandages and a bottle of water and stuffed them in the duffle bag as well. Tying her hair back in an elastic band, she went to her door. She pressed her ear against the wood, listening. She could hear the others speaking in calm tones. They sounded as if they were in the living room. She wouldn't be able to make it past them without being spotted. She'd have to find another way out.

She remembered that there was a towering rose trellis next to Mayhara's window. She knew the wood must have been strong for an object so tall; it had to be strong enough to hold her. Throwing on her jacket, she grabbed the duffle bag and headed for the door. Luckily, the doors in the temple didn't squeak or squeal, so she was able to open it without sound. She listened again to be sure no one was coming up the stairs, and then, with stealthy footsteps, she glided toward Mayhara's room.

Though Mayhara's door was closed, Huojin was relieved to find it wasn't locked. She didn't turn on the light, thankful the moon shone brightly enough through the window for her to maneuver through the room. Mayhara kept her room impeccably clean, her bed made so neatly one would think it had never been slept in. The few items Mayhara did bring with her to the temple were organized methodically on her dresser. To Huojin, these were signs of someone who was well put together. Someone who was secure in who they were and what they were doing. Confident in what they could contribute to a worthy cause.

Biting her lip, Huojin ignored the feeling of unworthiness rising inside her and raced to the window. After sliding it open, she peered outside to check the trellis. It was secured to the wall of the temple with steel clamps. Huojin's eyes went downward to estimate the height. If she fell, she'd surely be paralyzed. Luckily, her duffle bag had mostly clothes in it and nothing breakable. She hoisted it through the window and let it drop to the ground. Holding her breath, she listened for the impact, and then let out a sigh of relief after the *thump*. It hadn't been too loud; no one should have noticed.

Ducking her head, she shifted her body to climb through the window, reaching out her hand to grab a wooden beam of the trellis. When she felt it safe enough, she wriggled the rest of the way out and positioned herself fully on the trellis. She held back a yelp when a thorn from the rose vines pricked her arm, concentrating instead on making her way down as quickly and quietly as she could manage. Fear that Salina would go against her request and check in on her kept her moving. After a few more thorn pricks, Huojin finally made it to the ground. Without hesitation, she grabbed her duffle bag and darted for the cover of the woods.

She decided to follow the road down the mountain but kept out of sight under the cloak of the nearby trees. By the time she was halfway down, she was covered in sweat and out of breath. She paused by a tree stump and unzipped her duffle bag to retrieve her water, grateful that it hadn't been damaged when she'd dropped the bag from Mayhara's window.

After a few gulps of water and steadier breaths, Huojin continued her trek down the mountain. She wondered if anyone might have noticed she was gone. A deep, dark part of her wondered if Darshana would be glad she'd left.

Pushing away her discouraging thoughts, she picked up her pace and made it down to the main road. She knew there was a small town nearby. If she could somehow make it to a sub-train station, she'd be able to get far enough away that the other mages couldn't stop her and force her to come back.

It was a forty- minute walk to the town. The streets were relatively empty, since it was so late at night. Most of the small houses in the small town had dark windows, the people apparently turned in for the night. She followed the distant sound of a sub-train, knowing it would take her far away. She only hoped her heartache wouldn't follow her.

About twenty minutes later, she was relieved to find a sub-train station. She had no idea of where to go, but something inside her was driving her to go to the abandoned academy. No one would be there. And it used to be home to her. And maybe—just maybe—she'd find some peace.

There was no one at the station at first, just the moonlight gleaming off the tracks to hold her attention. A shadow moved, and she spotted a figure approaching the far end of the station. Her senses were on high alert, and she forced herself to steady her breathing. She checked the digital display to see it was a two-minute wait until the sub-train would arrive. The man didn't approach her. Instead, he remained at the far end, taking a seat on a bench. She told herself she was acting paranoid. No one knew she was here, and no one would think to find her in this small town. She stared at the digital display, counting down the time until the sub-train arrived.

When the sub-train pulled in, Huojin

inconspicuously watched the man at the far end of the station. He stood and boarded the train without looking her way. Breathing a sigh of relief, she stepped onto the train and slumped down into one of the seats, resting her weary bones on her duffelbag.

The property appeared to have been left untouched for years. Past the cast-iron fence, the remnants of the massive academy building stood in the moonlight. The Eradication had demolished most of the building, but what was left of it stood tall and proud, like the last remaining hope in a devastating war, a soldier that refused to give up.

Huojin shuddered. She didn't feel like such a soldier. Perhaps if she went in and felt the soul of the place, it might give her a last spark of hope.

The grounds, which had once been meticulously manicured and blossoming with life, were now scattered with rubble and weeds. A hare stood on its hind legs to watch her approach the main entrance before it scurried off into the darkness of a nearby field.

Her breaths were steady as she got closer to the school that had once been her home. She used to be proud, walking the halls of the palace, strutting onto the battlefield, receiving honors as one of the top golden mages in her house. But she felt none of that now. She pushed open the dilapidated doors of the front entrance and took a step inside.

"Lakshmi," she prayed with a whisper, "I'm lost."

She took deliberate steps, one foot in front of the other, hoping inspiration and faith would come to her. The tiles at her feet were destroyed and covered in dust, much resembling the feeling in her heart. Tears hung on her lashes as her heart ached.

"Lakshmi. Please."

She stopped in the middle of the foyer, closing her eyes and waiting. Perhaps her goddess would send her a sign, an answer. Huojin pressed her lips tightly together as her tears flowed freely over her cheeks. She could barely hold back the shudder of her shoulders as sobs threatened to crumple her to the ground.

A metallic *clink* sounded from somewhere behind her.

Her eyes shot wide open, and she stopped breathing so she could listen. Turning slowly and squinting against the darkness, she scanned the area, searching for the source of the sound. Had the hare from the field followed her inside? Perhaps it had knocked over a bit of tile in its travels?

She wanted to speak out, to ask who might be there. But what purpose would that serve? Unless it was one of the mages or Darshana, whoever might be there, whoever might have tracked her to this spot, could only serve as a danger.

Her heart pounded in her chest. A dark figure moved into a beam of moonlight. The figure moved slowly, carefully.

Huojin dropped her duffle bag and closed her hands into fists. She could barely feel the surge of golden energy in her palms. It was weak, but it was there.

"Ah," the figure said, moving closer into view. "So you're the golden elite."

Huojin gasped and looked down at her hands. The faint golden glow could be seen through her clenched fingers.

"Who are you?" she asked. "What do you want?"

"I see I have you at a disadvantage, me knowing who you are, but you not knowing who I am." The young man took three more steps until moonlight surrounded him. "We met before. But I can understand if you don't remember me. There was a lot going on at the time."

Huojin studied his face, her heart racing. He looked familiar, but she couldn't place him. When he shifted to adjust his fingerless, black leather gloves, she realized where she'd seen him.

"You're one of the dark mages."

Though tall and built of lean muscle, his face was almost boyish, with thick lips and a narrow chin. His eyes were half-concealed by this mane of dark brown hair, which stuck out from his head in one direction, as if it had been blown by a strong wind and frozen in place. He wore a black jacket with fur lining the collar, and the ends of his sleeves were a bright red that covered the wrists of his gloves.

Huojin held her chin up. "You shouldn't be here."

"You underestimate me. But that's because you don't know me. So let me introduce myself. My name is Avi. Avi Laghari. Perhaps you've heard of my father, Governor Laghari?"

Huojin's jaw dropped slightly. "You're the governor's son? And a dark mage?"

"It's typical, don't you think? With great power, blah blah blah."

Avi took another step toward her. She immediately fell into a defensive stance.

"Stay where you are." The faint glow remained in her palms as she held them up.

He let out a chuckle. "Or what? I can see you're injured. Your glow is weak. And you've been crying."

"You can go to hell. I'll fight you if I need to."

"You don't understand." Avi shifted his stance, as if ready to attack. "There's no hope for you. Kashmeru is bringing those faithful to him to the promised land. The rest of you are doomed. So you might as well give up now."

"Over my dead body."

He smirked. "Thanks for the invitation."

She felt the heat before anything else. But it wasn't fire that came at her. Not flames like she could produce. It was as if a wave of hot electricity coursed through the air at her. She could see the plumes of energy distorting the air, and then the pain hit her. She let out a cry as her body was pushed backward. Her palms glowed golden, and she found her bearings.

With a guttural shout, she pushed out her fire energy at him. Streams of golden flames shot toward him, the most she'd been able to generate since suffering her injuries.

The scowl on his face was illuminated by her fire. Avi shifted his arms dramatically, extending one above his head and the other out at his side. He then brought his hands together hard in a loud clap. The energy in the air shifted again, the waves catching Huojin's fire and ricocheting the flames back toward her.

With a gasp, she jumped to the side and tucked into a roll that brought her into a crouch.

"It doesn't have to be this way," Avi said, lowering his arms. "Join us and live forever. Pledge your fealty to Kashmeru and be saved."

"Never!"

Avi tilted his head and chuckled again. "Wrong answer, sweetie."

His arms shot out and whirled in a circular motion. Huojin jumped to her feet and pushed out her arms, palms facing him. But the glow in her hands faded as an explosion of distorted energy rippled through the air, buzzing around her until finally the ripple hit her, crushing her bones and ripping the life out of her.

Thirteen

Salina's heart was in her throat as she ran from Huojin's empty room to the office where Jae and Mayhara were working. For a second, she was afraid to speak. Afraid of what it might mean.

"Salina?" Jae asked when he looked up from the computer.

"Have you guys seen Huojin?" Salina wrung her hands.

Jae shook his head. "I haven't seen her all morning."

A wrinkle formed on Mayhara's forehead. "She's not in her room?"

"No. And her duffle bag is gone."

"She ran away?" Mayhara stood so fast, her chair skidded away behind her. "Why? Why would she abandon us?"

Salina raked a hand through her curls, her brows drawn together. "I think she was feeling the pressure. I think it was getting to her. We've got to find her!"

Shiro suddenly appeared behind Salina. The color had been drawn from his face.

"Wait, guys," he said. "I know where she is. Come see."

They all followed as he led them to the living room, where the news program had been paused on the televiewer. Darshana and Mr. Kitaro were on the couch, waiting for them. Shiro clicked a button on the remote, and the news program rewound by thirty seconds.

"—last night, where fans of the traditional festival performance were astonished at what appeared on stage. Warning: the images we're about to show you could be too

graphic for sensitive viewers."

On the screen, a video clip was shown of a small, outdoor stage at the Navratri festival. As the curtains opened, a form crumpled on the floor, center stage, was revealed. The crowd gasped and began to murmur, some of them fleeing the area in a panic. As the footage continued, the newscaster went on.

"… because the victim suffered multiple broken bones all over her body, officials believe that foul play was the cause of death. Authorities have since removed the body and taken it to the city's coroner's office for examination. Initial fingerprints have revealed that the victim to be Huojin Adachi, who has recently been reported missing by her employer at Fukuhara Systems, Incorporated. One of Miss Adachi's co-workers, who happened to be attending the festival and was close to the victim, stepped forward to speak to the Imperial Police and has speculated the victim's death to be linked to a jealous boyfriend…"

The corner of the screen displayed Huojin's picture. Salina's hands flew to her mouth, her eyes wide and filling with tears.

"No," Mayhara said, her voice barely audible. "No, it can't be."

"This wasn't some jealous boyfriend," Jae said. "It was the Pishacha."

Shiro rubbed at his jaw. "They left her body in a public place to send a message."

"Sick, pathetic animals," Mr. Kitaro said with clenched teeth.

"No." Salina shook her head, tears flowing down her cheeks. "No. I… I don't believe it. How could she be—? No. How did this happen?"

Mayhara went to her and enveloped her in her arms, stroking Salina's hair as she sobbed. "I'm so sorry."

Salina backed away from her, her eyes wide. "We've got to go get her."

Mayhara blanched. "What?"

"Her… body. Her corpse." Salina bit her lip. "We can't just leave her for the government to do who-knows-what to. We've got to take it from the coroner's office."

"That's a bad idea," Darshana said, not meeting anyone's gaze.

"What?" Salina scoffed.

Darshana raised her chin, her lips in a frown. "They'll be expecting that."

"She's right." Jae crossed his arms and squeezed at his chin. "That's why they left her in a public place. They knew it would make the media channels and we'd find out. They're betting on us wanting to get to her body. It's a trap."

"Jae." Salina's voice cracked. "We have to."

"It's a trap, Salina," Darshana reiterated.

"I don't care. We owe it to her." Salina straightened her shoulders. "We need to find a way. We can't leave her body in their hands." She turned to Shiro, locking gazes with him. "Please. She was my best friend."

Shiro clenched his jaw, studying Salina's face. His eyes then went to Jae, who searched the faces of the rest of the group. Darshana let out a sigh and dropped her head.

"All right." Jae placed a hand on Salina's shoulder. "Of course. We'll do whatever we can."

Salina nodded, wiping her tears away. "Thank you."

Jae and Shiro sprinted ahead through the confetti-covered streets, well ahead of Salina and Mayhara. Darshana followed somewhere behind. Mayhara had to trust that the guru would keep up. The coroner's office was located two blocks away from the main street where the festival was taking place. It was still early in the day, and the streets weren't full yet. But between the handful of patrons, stand workers, and performers practicing for their shows, there was enough of a cover to keep the focus off the mages' mission.

Jae almost stumbled as he threw his back against the wall of a building. He signaled for the others to keep out of sight. As Mayhara caught up, she spotted the two Imperial Police officers making their rounds near the building housing the coroner's office.

Pushing a sweet-bun cart, an elderly man strolled along, most likely hoping for some early sales. His bright orange umbrella was big enough to create some cover, so the group headed toward him.

"Easy now," Shiro whispered. "Don't draw attention."

The elderly man stopped as they approached,

displaying a friendly smile, despite the fact that he was missing some teeth. "Fancy some sweet buns?" he asked. "Buy two, get one free!"

"Sure." Jae pulled out his Linq and showed the screen to the vendor. "We'll take three."

The vendor used his scanning device to receive Jae's payment, all the while oblivious to the fact that Shiro and Salina were scanning the street for more police. Darshana's eyes darted back and forth as she accepted the bag of sweet buns.

"It looks clear," Salina said. "We should go in now."

A loud bang sounded in the air, causing everyone to turn their attention toward the main street. When a pink puff of smoke billowed up from a group of partygoers, Mayhara's shoulders relaxed.

"Just some kids goofing around," Shiro said.

"Okay, let's—" Salina froze, her words gone.

Mayhara turned to see three Pishacha standing in front of the coroner's office. Their eyes were like black coals above their mouth masks, glaring at the mages.

"Shit," Jae mumbled. "We've got to get out of here."

"No." Salina shook Mayhara's hand off her arm. "We can fight them. We need to get in there and get Huojin."

"We'll draw the attention of the police," Darshana said. "And there are far too many officials here. We'll all be arrested on the spot."

"Darshana's right." Jae put his hands together, pleading with her. "Even if we got through the Pishacha and the first pair of police, there'll just be more following. This place is crawling with them."

The three Pishacha began marching their way.

"Come on." Mayhara put her arm around Salina. "We've got to go."

"We can't leave her!" Salina cried.

"We have no choice," Darshana said. "I'm sorry."

"No. This isn't right."

The Pishacha picked up their pace.

Shiro grabbed Salina's arm. "Let's go!"

As they began to run, Mayhara's palms and bracelet glowed a crimson red. She only glanced behind her for a second, pushing her palm in the direction of the Pishacha. The pavement beneath the Pishacha shifted with such force, a huge block of earth rammed through the street, blocking their path.

"Go!" Jae yelled.

The five of them charged back toward the alley they'd

used to get to the street. Jae checked over his shoulder to make sure they'd all kept up. Mayhara grabbed the guru's arm and pulled her along so she wouldn't get left behind. When they reached the main street, they swerved around an enormous fountain that decorated the town square. As the Pishacha emerged from the alley, Shiro threw out copper energy, not halting his stride as he did so. The fountain burst, hard streams of water shooting out in every direction and knocking the Pishacha down.

"Go, go, go," Mayhara urged, knowing their car was just a street away.

They slipped through another alley, and this time Mayhara used her power to rattle the earth behind them. The buildings lining the alley shifted, bricks and stones getting knocked out of place, crumbling down into the alley into a huge mountain of debris.

Jae was the first to reach the car. The five of them were heaving breaths and quick limbs as they clambered into the car and took off.

No one spoke for a good fifteen minutes. They were already on the main highway when Salina began to cry.

"Salina." Mayhara put a hand on her arm.

"I've failed her," Salina said.

No one said anything. As they continued to drive toward the temple, Mayhara felt as if they had all failed Huojin. They'd failed her the moment she'd decided to leave the temple in the first place. If only she had noticed how desperate Huojin had been, if only she could have spoken with her and reassured her that they were on her side, maybe she wouldn't have felt the need to run away.

By the time they got back to the temple, everyone's spirits were low. Salina had stopped crying, but everything about her stance and expression told Mayhara there was a storm brewing underneath. When they got inside, Mayhara caught up with her, squeezing her shoulder.

"Salina, Huojin would never blame you."

Salina shook her head. "I don't know what to think anymore."

Darshana, who appeared behind her, folded her hands together. "It's best to not dwell on it, as nothing can change what's happened. What we need now is to get you ready."

Salina blinked, her brow creased. "Get me ready for what?"

"You are now the elite golden mage," Darshana said.

Salina turned to Mayhara.

"She's right," Mayhara said. "You're next in line."

Salina's mouth opened as if to speak, but she could only shake her head.

"We are all mourning the loss of Huojin," Darshana said gently. "But we cannot lose sight of the fact we have a universe to save. This is our life's mission, and we must adhere to our cause."

Salina stared at Darshana for a moment, and then she turned and grabbed at her own chest. Bent over slightly, she dragged in ragged breaths.

Mayhara rushed to her. "Are you all right?"

"No." Salina shook her head and rubbed at her throat. "My heart hurts. I can't breathe. It's as if the temple is falling in on me."

"Try to relax your thoughts," Darshana urged.

"*Relax my thoughts*?" Salina stood up straight and pointed a finger at her. "This is all your fault, you know. You pushed her too hard. You wouldn't let her stop forgetting that she wasn't living up to your expectations."

"They are not my expectations," Darshana said sternly. "It was her responsibility as part of the empire."

"But we're still people with feelings." Salina's fists

tightened. "I think you've mistaken us for robots."

Darshana bowed her head and pressed her lips together. "Perhaps you're right. Perhaps I did push her too hard. All of you. I, too, am feeling the pressure of this great responsibility. I didn't mean for this to happen."

"Well, it's too late to be thinking about how your words and actions can affect someone now." Salina's voice cracked. "She's gone."

The room echoed with her voice. Salina picked up a nearby vase and threw it across the room, where it shattered into a hundred pieces. With a frustrated grunt, Salina turned on her heel and stomped out of the room.

Mayhara glanced at Darshana, who was still staring at the ground. "Don't worry. It's grief that's driving her right now. I'll talk to her, but she's going to need some time."

"I want to say I understand," Darshana said. "But time is one thing we don't have a lot of."

Fourteen

Naree blinked. She couldn't remember how she got to where she was standing. The water in the sink splashed as it flowed from the faucet, and her hands were covered in blood.

Another death.

Lakshmi, the pure goddess of light whose soul was her own, was crying out inside of her.

What have I done? This is wrong.

Naree glanced at the mirror. Tears stained her cheeks. Every death was adding up and weighing her down. It was as if she could feel each of the victim's souls pass through her as they died. She felt their pain, their agony. Inside her, Lakshmi was weeping as well.

My love, Kashmeru spoke. *Do not give up on me. We're so close.*

Her breath shuddered as she washed the blood off her hands. She nodded as she held back a whimper.

Are you still with me, my love?

She pressed her lips together and then forced a small smile. She nodded again, her head spinning. "Yes. Yes, I'm with you."

Fifteen

Jae stared at the screen of his Linq, a wrinkle etched in his brow. It took him a second to realize who was calling him. He walked to his window and glanced up at the night sky as he held the Linq to his ear.

"Yes?"

"Hello. This is Nian from the scroll shop. You asked me to contact you about the content of a scroll."

"Nian, yes, of course."

The line was quiet for a moment, and Jae wondered if they'd been disconnected.

"We heard about the body left in the city square," Nian said. "I assume it was a… friend of yours. An elite mage."

Jae stiffened. "That's none of your concern."

"We think it is. It tells us what could happen to those in your circle. And by us helping you, we might be considered part of that circle."

The mark in the sky noting the comet's position caught Jae's eye. "Did you call to tell me that you no longer wish to help?"

"No. We have some information on what the other scroll is. We have contacted our great-aunt. She says she might know of the map that's on it."

"We can't be sure it's a map. We've studied it and can't match a location."

"Think on a smaller scale," Nian said. "We think this is a more specific map. Of a place somewhere hidden. Perhaps underground."

"How can we be sure?"

"Bring the scroll in. Next week, Wednesday. Our great-aunt will be in town then and can take a look at it."

Jae rubbed at his chin. "I don't know if we have that much time."

"That's all I can offer you."

"Fine. We'll be there."

Jae marked the date of the meeting in his Linq and slipped the device back into his pocket. He thought about waiting until the morning to tell Mayhara, but part of him was glad he had a reason to see her again before he turned in for the night.

Running a hand through his hair, he headed out of his room and down the hall. He straightened his shirt before knocking on her door.

Mayhara opened her door, surprised to see Jae standing there. She might have been imagining it, but she could have sworn there was a reddish tint to his cheeks.

"Hey," he said. "Did I interrupt you?"

She followed his glance to the Linq in her hand. "Oh. No, sorry. I was checking for more news."

"Find anything?"

"No. Just the usual." She walked over to her dresser and placed her Linq on it. "What's up?"

"I just got a call from Nian about the scroll. He said they have a great-aunt who might be able to tell us what it is."

"That's great."

"He wants me to come by next week so she can take a look at it. I thought you'd like to come."

"Yeah, Count me in."

"Great." He tapped his fingertips against the doorframe as he studied her face. "Hey, are you all right?"

"Yeah. I think I'm still processing it all. This whole thing with Huojin got me thinking about my family."

"Darshana said she got them transferred under a different name. They won't connect them with you. They should be safe."

"For now."

"We'll get them out."

"You can't promise me that." She shook her head and sighed. "I wouldn't ask it of you."

He took two steps into her room and held out his hand. "Come here," he said softly.

Though she was taken aback by his request, she

reached out and took his hand. He pulled her closer and wrapped his arms around her. She didn't question his intentions, but instead let herself take comfort in his warm embrace.

"We'll be okay," he whispered. "We're in this together, remember?"

She pressed her head against his chest. "Yes. I remember."

He kissed the top of her head. Goosebumps sprung to life all over her body.

"Goodnight, Mayha," he said, using the shortened version of her name she'd only ever heard from her parents.

"Goodnight."

He backed away slowly, his eyes still on her as he gently released her. She smiled, but her vulnerability caused her to wrap her arms around herself. With a nod, Jae turned and disappeared out her door.

As his footfalls dissipated, Mayhara closed her bedroom door and pressed her back against it. Without thinking, she touched the spot on the top of her head where Jae had kissed her. The hint of a smile formed on her lips as she brought her fingers to her mouth. She suddenly felt hot, as if someone had turned up the heat in her room to full blast. She blew out a breath and headed for her window. Maybe she just needed some air.

When she slid her window open, she spotted movement in the trees nearby.

Salina?

Mayhara leaned out to get a better look, but Salina—if that was who it was—sprinted too quickly through the trees. Without hesitation, Mayhara grabbed her Linq, darted out of her room, and hurried down the stairs, thankful she hadn't yet taken off her shoes. Everyone must have been in their rooms, because she didn't spot anyone downstairs. Her heart began to race as she ran outside and in the direction she'd seen Salina go. She wasn't sure what she was up to, but she guessed it had something to do with Huojin. Would she really be venturing out to retrieve her body? What was her plan, exactly? Even if she took the train, how would she bring Huojin's body back to the temple? Besides, it was too dangerous for one mage to go wandering off alone in the middle of the night. And with Salina's fragile emotional state, Mayhara had even more reason to worry.

Mayhara used her mage powers of stability to keep

her balance as she maneuvered through the trees and underbrush, chasing Salina. She could feel Salina's footsteps through her connection with the earth, making it easier for her to catch up.

"Salina!" she called when she caught sight of her.

Salina's shoulders tensed as she skidded to a stop. Her golden-highlighted curls swung around her head as she turned to face Mayhara. There was a wild look in her eyes that gave Mayhara pause.

"Where are you going?" Mayhara asked between bated breaths.

Salina stared at Mayhara, inhaling and exhaling so hard it moved her entire body. "If Darshana's not going to take responsibility for Huojin's body, I'm not going to sit back and do nothing."

"Salina, it's too dangerous. Huojin wouldn't have wanted you to put yourself in danger."

"You didn't know her like I did. Nobody did. She wouldn't have wanted to be abandoned like this. I can't just leave her there and forget about it."

"No one's asking you to forget." Mayhara stepped closer. "We just can't risk any more lives."

"Don't you get it? She's worth the risk. Nothing you

say will change my mind. I owe this to her."

Mayhara held her hands up, signaling that she wasn't going to argue with her. "Okay. Okay. Then… at least let me go with you. Let me help you get her body. I can't let you do this alone."

Salina took a long, deep breath in through her nose and blew it out her mouth, her eyes studying Mayhara.

"Fine. But I'm not waiting. I've got to hurry to the next sub-train station. We need to move now before they dispose of her body disrespectfully."

"Okay. But how about we drive? Or did you have another plan on how we're going to bring Huojin back here?"

Forty-five minutes later, Mayhara parked the car near the city center. She didn't think it was the best idea to be out near the festival again, but she didn't know any other way to make sure Salina didn't suffer the same fate as Huojin.

The square was much more crowded now than it had been when they'd been there earlier. People attending the festival were dressed in traditional garb, the red, yellow, green, black, and blue of their *Ghagra choli* and *kurta* clothes reflected in the street decoration. Loud music played as festival performers showcased traditional dances. Judging by the jovial looks on everyone's faces, one would never suspect the end the world might be nearing.

Salina rushed from the car and began zigzagging through the crowd.

"Salina, wait!" Mayhara had to push through patrons to catch up with her.

She wasn't sure Salina had even heard her, for Salina didn't stop, didn't hesitate. She carried on as if she were drawn to the coroner's office by a powerful magnet. There were too many people getting in Mayhara's way. She knew better not to use her powers where there were so many witnesses, but she had to stop Salina before something bad happened. Discreetly pulling up her powers, she quickly aimed energy at Salina to throw her off-balance. Because it was tight quarters, a handful of patrons near Salina also lost their footing. To anyone else, it would have appeared as if the lot of them had accidentally bumped into each other and stumbled. But Salina knew the cause of the disturbance. As she found her bearings, she glanced back at Mayhara with a squared jaw. Mayhara quickly closed the distance between them and put a hand on her elbow.

"I said we'd do this together," Mayhara said. "Please trust me."

Salina raised a brow. "You didn't have to trip me."

"Apparently, I did."

Salina bit her cheek. "Okay, fine. Let's go."

"What is your plan, exactly?" Mayhara walked beside Salina, trying to keep up with her pace. "How are we going to get in?"

"I'm going to set off the fire alarm. Someone's bound to open the door once that goes off."

"And draw attention from the police and fire brigade? I don't think that's going to work."

Salina pursed her lips. "Fine. Plan B. I'll short-circuit the lock pad. My brother showed me how to do it once."

"Once? Have you ever done it yourself?"

Salina gave her a sideways glance. "There's a first time for everything."

Mayhara looked around, scanning the crowd for Imperial Police or Pishacha. Festivalgoers danced through the square, the choreography extremely enthusiastic and energetic. Everyone was caught up in the fun. No one paid Mayhara or Salina any attention.

There was still no sign of Imperial Police or the Pishacha when they reached the door of the coroner's office. From what Mayhara could see through the narrow windows flanking the door, the lights were off inside the building. She was relieved by the thought that the office was closed for the day, but she wasn't about to release the breath she was holding quite yet. There were still too many eyes around, and some of them could have been watching them from the shadows.

Salina set her hand on the lock pad. Her palm emitted a golden glow.

"What are you doing?" Mayhara shifted her position to block the view of the lock pad from passersby.

"I'm overheating the circuits." Salina's glow grew brighter. "This will cause the system to crash and shut down temporarily. It will take three seconds for the emergency power generator to reboot the system, so that means—"

The red light of the lock pad went out as a beep sounded. Salina grabbed Mayhara's arm with one hand and pushed the door open with the other.

"Three. Two."

The door closing behind them took the place of

Salina's count of *one*.

"Where, exactly, did your brother learn that?" Mayhara whispered.

"Let's just concentrate on one crime at a time, okay?"

As Mayhara's eyes widened, Salina let out a small laugh. Though Mayhara was still curious about Salina's hotwiring, she was somewhat comforted to see her smile again.

"I'm kidding." Salina urged Mayhara forward, behind the main desk, and toward the door marked *Examiner*. "He's studying electronics at university."

They both stopped in front of the beveled-glass window of the door, and Salina's mouth turned down into a frown.

"Do you think…" Salina let out a trembling breath. "She's in there?"

"We've come all this way." Mayhara placed a hand on Salina's shoulder and gave her a gentle squeeze. "Let's find out."

Sixteen

They used the glow of their palms to light the way. The door creaked as they opened it. Mayhara was hit with the smell of formaldehyde, causing her to flinch and blink rapidly.

Salina extended her arms, holding them high to illuminate a greater area of the room. Two bare, metal examination tables stood four feet apart from each other in the center of the room. One wall of the room was lined, floor to ceiling, with dull, metal cabinets, each displaying a row of labeled square doors.

Salina went to the cabinets and leaned closer, reading the labels. Mayhara stood beside her, searching for Huojin's name.

"There," Mayhara said. Stunned to actually see Huojin's name on the door, she couldn't find the strength to point.

Salina followed her gaze, her breath hitching when she spotted her friend's name. Her shaking hand reached for the electronic button next to the label. Her finger hovered there for what seemed like an eternity. With a visible swallow, she pushed the button.

A beep sounded, and the drawer slid out. White, frosty mist escaped from within the drawer, dancing above a pristine white sheet covering a form below it.

Salina chewed at her cheek, hesitating before reaching for a corner of the sheet. A freezing chill traveled along Mayhara's skin as Salina slowly peeled the cover back to reveal Huojin's blueish face. Salina's knees gave out, and she grabbed on to Mayhara for support. Mayhara had to close her eyes and muster her strength to keep from falling herself.

She was really dead. It wasn't a trick. Though Huojin's skin was blue and her features seemed to have sunken in a bit, Mayhara knew it was her corpse, kept frozen in a mortuary cabinet until her autopsy could be completed.

"Do you think they've done anything with her yet?" Salina asked, her voice a soft whisper. "She doesn't look cut into or anything."

Mayhara shook her head. "I don't know."

"If the Pishacha are involved, maybe they haven't planned on examining her at all. They already know what killed her."

"Probably. They might be keeping her here just to cover—"

A click sounded from outside the room. A muffled voice could be heard on a radio transmitter.

"The police!" Mayhara quickly pushed the button on the drawer door. As Huojin's body slid back into the cabinet, Mayhara grabbed Salina's hand. "We've got to go."

"But—"

"We're going to end up in the drawers next to her if we don't get out of here. Come on!"

They raced to the back of the room to another door. Mayhara hoped it led to a way out instead of just a closet or storage area. They needed to find a way out of the building without getting caught.

The door opened to darkness, but when Mayhara pushed out crimson energy into her palm, the red glow revealed a hallway in front of them.

"We must have triggered a silent alarm." Mayhara pulled Salina along, hoping the hall led to an exit.

Salina threw a spark out that traveled down the hall. Before it fizzled out, Mayhara spotted a couple of places where the corridor branched out. She had no idea of the layout of the building, but she would have to take a chance that they'd pick the right hall.

As they raced down the corridor, a loud bang sounded behind them. A thin, red beam of light shone over Salina's shoulder.

"Stop right there!"

Mayhara gathered her powers and aimed a shot at their pursuers, knocking them off-balance. The red beam shifted upward and disappeared from their sight. Mayhara picked up her pace, but her grasp on Salina slipped as they reached the first turnoff in the corridor.

Mayhara practically dived to the right, grateful when she spotted the exit sign at the end of the corridor.

But when she glanced beside her, Salina wasn't there. Mayhara skidded to a stop and swirled around, frantically searching for her friend. A glowing blast of fire caused her to shield her eyes. As she backed up, trying to adjust to the change of light, she caught sight of an Imperial Police officer swinging a baton across the back of Salina's head. She crumpled to the ground. Mayhara slapped a hand over her mouth to keep from screaming and backed up against the wall behind a stack of boxes.

The beam from a tactical streamlight shown down the hall. Mayhara backed up even more and held her breath. Her heart was beating so hard, she thought the police would hear it for sure. When the light disappeared, she listened.

"Is someone else there?" one of the officers asked. "I thought there were two."

"Are you sure, Rico? I only saw one."

"Could have been her shadow," Rico said. "Okay, let's get her upstairs and contact Bhutano. Find out what he wants done with her."

Mayhara heard more footsteps and muffled voices.

Backup had arrived, which meant the police had been informed. She wasn't sure she could take on all of them, and chances were that more officers would arrive. She couldn't make a move. Not yet.

She pressed herself hard against the wall until the voices and shuffling of feet disappeared. Her heartbeat pounding in her throat made it hard for her to breathe properly. When it was finally quiet, she whipped out her Linq and pressed Jae's contact button.

"Mayhara?"

She was relieved to hear his voice. "Jae. They have Salina."

"Wha—Where are you?"

"At the coroner's office."

"What? Why? Didn't we just agree how dangerous that is?"

"Jae, there's no time to argue. The police took her. But they said they're bringing her upstairs and contacting Bhutano. They're not arresting her. If I can find her before—"

"No! No, don't move. Are you hidden?"

"Not for long." Mayhara peered down the dark hallway. "I'm sure this place will be flooded with police and Pishacha soon."

"Get out and find a place to hide. Shiro and I are on the way. Wait for us. You can't take them on alone."

Mayhara didn't answer. Could she really wait for Jae and Shiro? What if Bhutano showed up before they got there? If there was a chance to somehow save Salina, get her out of wherever they were holding her, she didn't think she could wait.

"Mayhara!"

"Right," she said, not wanting him to argue with him. "Hurry."

She pressed the END CALL button and tucked her Linq away, sinking to the floor as she tried to control her heavy breaths.

The silence of the hall pressed in on her. She turned her head toward the exit sign. She could easily break out of the building and find a place to hide and wait for Jae and Shiro. But was that the right thing to do?

Mayhara stood and clenched her fists. Time was not on their side. It would take Jae and Shiro at least half an hour to get to them, even on his impeccably fast motorcycle. By then, who knew what might have happened to Salina. They'd already lost one friend. They couldn't bear to lose another.

Mayhara stretched out her neck and shoulders, preparing herself. She'd do what she could to avoid being spotted, but she had to be ready, just in case.

She hadn't spotted any stairs on her way into the building, but maybe there was an elevator entrance she'd passed without noticing. Retracing her steps, she continued down the corridor toward the coroner's office. The rooms she passed seemed to be laboratories and other offices. Between two of the doors, a fire extinguisher was mounted on the wall, and beside it, a fire escape plan. According to the plan, she wasn't too far away from the elevators. But being trapped in one and cornered by the police or the Pishacha was not going to be beneficial when it came to finding Salina. Instead, Mayhara opted for the stairs.

The first two upper floors led to more labs and offices and one giant computer room. When she arrived at the fourth floor, the hallway was lit up. Mayhara backed up from the stairwell door and listened for movement or voices. The doors on this floor were closed, and the hall appeared empty.

"Here goes nothing," she whispered to herself as she

eased out into the hall.

Stealthily moving from room to room, she found a filing room among some offices. As she continued down the hall, she came upon a wall of windows. A giant oval-shaped conference table took up the majority of the floor space. She was about to breeze past the room until she spotted a 3D image of the Akutake comet up on a viewing screen. She glanced around at the rest of the freeze frame, noting the star-filled sky at the top of the image. At the bottom of the screen was an illustration of what appeared to be a tunnel leading down into a cavern. The entire image mesmerized her. She immediately pushed open the door and entered the conference room, searching for the projector that shone the image onto the screen. Up near the ceiling, the beamer was mounted on a shelf, but the wires connected to it went behind the wall. She didn't see a computer anywhere, but there was a remote at one end of the table.

Checking over her shoulder to make sure no one was in the hall, she rushed over to the remote and pushed the *play* button. The video began to play, but there was no sound. She concluded that someone had turned the speakers off when they'd left the room but hadn't bothered to turn off the computer or the beamer. She couldn't understand what she was watching, so she hit the *rewind* button and played the clip from the beginning.

There were no words on the screen explaining anything, so she had to pay attention to try to figure out what the clip was about. The 3D animation showed the comet coursing through the sky over what appeared to be the horizon of the Earth. At one point, the horizon highlighted the tunnel that led to some kind of cavern. The video image then displayed lines that must have represented vibrations from the comet growing and reaching the cavern.

Mayhara stopped the video and played it again. She couldn't figure out where this cavern might have been or what the significance of the vibrations reaching it meant. Her head spun with confusion, and she knew she had to continue searching for Salina, so she took out her Linq and played the video again, this time capturing the whole thing with her camera.

She slipped out of the room and looked up and down the hall again. There was still no sign of any police or Pishacha, but she knew the clock was ticking. After checking a few more rooms and finding nothing, she began to lose hope. She was about to give up when she came upon a locked door. All the other doors had been unlocked, which made Mayhara suspect this one had something to hide. Hopefully, it would be Salina.

She pressed her ear against the door but didn't hear anything or anyone inside. Pulling on her mage powers, she felt through the floor, her connection to the gravel in the concrete allowing her to sense if anyone might be behind the door. She could sense the weight of something or someone in the corner of the room, but she couldn't be sure if it was even a person, let alone Salina.

She desperately wanted to knock and call out to her friend, but if it wasn't her, if it was someone else, or if what she felt was an object, like a couch that weighed as much as a person, and someone heard her, she'd be caught for sure.

Her Linq vibrated. She slipped it out to check the screen, but just as she caught a glimpse of Jae's message to sit tight, the elevator down the hall dinged. Mayhara swiftly put her phone away and took a defensive stance. She tried to ignore the weak feeling in her legs and the sensation of suffocation. She couldn't afford to be afraid.

The three police officers who emerged from the

elevator charged at her, one of them pulling a gun. Mayhara ignored their protests and shouting, shooting crimson energy balls at them. One guard was knocked back by the energy ball, his head cracking as it impacted with the wall. The guard with the gun shot at Mayhara, but she quickly formed a crimson shield that blocked the bullet, propelling it off to the side. Mayhara used her stability powers to throw off the remaining guards' balance, but one of them was charging at her so fast that even with the shift of balance, he managed to careen into her, knocking her back onto the floor. By the time she got her wits about her, the other guard had approached and drawn his cyber baton. Its head buzzed as the guard held it near her ear.

"Move and I tear this through your face," he said.

Mayhara's heavy breathing and the buzz of the cyber baton was all that could be heard for a good minute. The guard who'd shot at her grabbed her by the arm and pulled her to her feet.

"Throw her in with the other one," he said. "Looks like Bhutano gets two instead of one."

Her arm was pinched in the guard's grasp. The other kept the cyber baton dangerously near her head. She had no choice; she had to do as they said. The only silver lining was that they would take her directly to Salina.

They dragged her to a room at the end of the hall. Mayhara kept an eye on the lock pad as the guard punched the code in, dropping her gaze when he checked her face.

"Secure her like the other," he said once they'd gotten into the room. "We don't want her escaping."

Pain erupted in her wrist bones as electro-cuffs were secured around her wrists behind her back. The other guard pushed her into a chair and tied a black rope he'd unhooked from his belt loop around Mayhara's midsection. He sneered at her as they backed away and out of the room.

As soon as the door closed, Mayhara scanned the room. It appeared to be some kind of informal meeting room, with two short couches facing each other and the chair Mayhara was tied to next to a small table. Just past one of the couches, Mayhara spotted feet.

"Salina!"

Salina's body sagged against the floor. She was tied with the same rope as Mayhara, but to the leg of a small end table. Mayhara bounced in the chair, moving it enough to get a better look at her. Salina's head was bent at a strange angle against the end table. Mayhara could only hope she was still alive.

"Salina! Salina! Wake up!" Mayhara reached out with her powers and made the floor below Salina quake.

A moan escaped Salina's lips as she slowly sat up. Mayhara released a quick breath of relief. She was alive. Her wrists were also locked in electro-cuffs. She looked up at Mayhara, and then her eyes widened.

Thank the gods!

Salina shifted, trying to look behind her. "What happened?"

"They hit you from behind. They're working with the Pishacha. Bhutano is on his way. We've got to get out of here."

Salina looked down at the black rope around her chest. Narrowing her eyes, she glared at the rope. A thin trail of fire energy emerged, traveling from behind her where her hands were trapped. Salina guided the fire trail to the rope. Gold cinders burned through the rope and smoke wafted up into Salina's face. Salina guided the fire trail to the rope. Gold cinders burned through the rope and smoke wafted up into Salina's face. As soon as the ropes fell away, she stretched, wriggling to her feet with her wrists still cuffed behind her. She hurried to Mayhara's side.

"I'm going to burn your rope. It's better if I'm touching them, which means I have to turn around and do it behind my back. Let me know if I get too close. I don't want to burn you."

"Okay." Mayhara moved her head back just in case.

Salina's fingers felt the rope, and her palm emitted a golden glow.

"Jae and Shiro are on the way," Mayhara said as the rope began to burn. She tried not to think about how close Salina's fire was coming to her body. "And I know the keycode. But we're both stuck in these electro-cuffs."

Salina looked toward the door as Mayhara's ropes fell away. "Even if we managed to get the door open, we'd be at a disadvantage out there in these cuffs."

Mayhara shrugged, her shoulders slumping. "I'm sorry."

Salina backed onto the arm of the couch. "It should be me apologizing. I'm the one who got us into this. And I couldn't even save Huojin's body."

They were quiet for a moment, reflecting on their

situation.

"If only I had known how she was feeling," Mayhara began. "I didn't realize she felt like running away."

"I think it was more than that. I knew she was feeling the pressure," Salina said. "But I didn't know how much she was suffering."

"She would forgive you, you know?"

"I guess I need to step up now," Salina said with a nod. "I'm the golden elite. Going forward and playing my part to win this war is what I have to concentrate on now."

Footfalls sounded in the hall. Salina and Mayhara jumped to their feet. Though their hands were still trapped behind their backs, they took defensive stances. It would be a tricky fight, but they weren't about to give up yet.

The hall echoed with a couple of thumps and what sounded like people falling to the floor. Mayhara and Salina exchanged glances, shifting their balances in case the door opened.

"Check those rooms. I'll check these." It was Jae's voice.

Mayhara gasped and ran to the door, Salina in tow.

"Jae! Shiro! We're in here!"

Mayhara kicked the door a few times to get their attention.

"We're here!" Salina added.

"Mayhara? Salina?" came Jae's voice from the other side of the door.

"Yes!" Mayhara pressed her forehead on the door. "The lock pad. The code is 468225."

She and Salina stepped back as they heard Jae punching the numbers in. With a final beep, the door clicked open. Mayhara couldn't help the smile that appeared on her face when she saw Jae standing there.

He placed his hands on Mayhara's shoulders. "Are you all right?" His eyes went from her to Salina, but his hands remained on Mayhara.

"Yeah, but we're cuffed," she said.

Behind him in the hall, Shiro bent down over a body sprawled on the floor. With a smirk, Shiro stood, producing a set of keys.

"I found something," Mayhara said as Shiro unlocked her cuffs. "Something to do with the comet and some cavern. I took a video with my Linq."

Salina shook out her hands after Shiro unlocked her.

"Okay," Jae said. "We'll have to wait until we're out of here to look at it. There's a hoard of Imperial Police downstairs. Shiro and I managed to evade them until we got up here and ran into this one." He pointed to the officer on the floor. "But we can't risk taking the elevator or the stairs down."

"Though they are a little busy with a flooding problem at the moment." Shiro gave everyone a wink. "But what about the fire escape?"

"Exactly what I was thinking," Salina said.

Seventeen

$\mathcal{J}$ae couldn't stop checking the rearview mirror of his motorcycle. They'd made their escape seemingly unnoticed. The cacophony and throng of the celebration had offered enough cover for them to make it down the fire escape, through the mass of partygoers, and to the safety of their vehicles unscathed and unnoticed.

Jae was glad when Shiro had offered to drive Salina in

the car. She had been too distraught about Huojin to drive, and Jae needed Mayhara near him. He hadn't said so out loud, but if Shiro hadn't taken the initiative and proposed to drive Salina, Jae would have insisted. He would have found a way to keep Mayhara with him.

Jae had panicked when Mayhara had called him for help, as if the walls had been crashing in on him and his heart would thrash through his chest. Now that he'd found her, he didn't want to let her out of his sight. They were elbows-deep in the middle of a war, but as long as Mayhara's arms were wrapped around him and they weren't being followed, everything would be all right.

When they got back to the temple, Jae didn't want her to let go. As he set his kickstand down, her hands slipped off his waist, and he held back a frown. He couldn't help but stare at her as she pulled off her helmet and handed it to him.

"Thanks," she said when he took it.

"You okay?" He set both helmets on the bike.

She nodded but wrapped her arms around herself. "Shaken up. I hope Salina's all right."

"Me too." He knew he was staring, but he couldn't tear his eyes away. It was taking every ounce of willpower he had not to pull her into his arms. "Mayhara…"

She watched his face, her brows drawn together. "What is it?"

The lights of the car Shiro drove lit up the carport as it approached.

"Jae, what's wrong?" Mayhara asked.

Taking a step closer, he reached out to her. He opened his mouth but couldn't put his feelings into words. Not now. Not here. "You, uh, you've got some dirt on your face."

His eyes still locked with hers, he gently brushed her cheek with his thumb.

Her lips parted.

"Hey," Shiro called, walking over from the car with Salina. "Everyone all right?"

Mayhara cleared her throat and turned to him. "Yeah. Salina, how are you?"

Salina's gaze was trained on the ground. She gave a shrug. "I don't know. I know we had to get out of there, but it feels so disrespectful to just… leave her there."

"We tried, Salina." Mayhara held her hands. "There was nothing else we could have done."

Tears began to flow down Salina's cheeks. Mayhara

let out a sympathetic whimper and pulled Salina in for hug.

"Let's go inside," Shiro said. "I can make us some tea if you'd like."

Salina nodded, backing out of Mayhara's arms and wiping her cheeks. "That sounds nice. Thanks. Maybe it will help with this headache."

"You were hit pretty hard," Mayhara said. "You probably should ice it."

"Oh, that I can definitely help with." Shiro held his palm out to Salina, and the copper glow was soon covered with a small block of ice.

For the first time that day, Salina smiled.

❧

They'd fallen asleep in the living room, their half-drunken tea now cold on the coffee table. Darshana cleared her throat, and Mayhara opened her eyes. Her head was resting on Jae's chest. She didn't remember falling asleep in that position, but she wasn't complaining.

"What time is it?" Mayhara sat up and squinted at the sun coming in through the windows.

"Nearly noon," Darshana answered. "When did you get back?"

Jae stretched, blinking as he woke. "In the middle of the night. I guess we fell asleep."

Salina shifted, pressing her hands against her temples, and Shiro yawned loudly.

Mr. Kitaro appeared behind Darshana, sipping a coffee. "Good morning. You all look better than I expected. I can't tell you how tempted I was to call the police about a possible kidnapping. Luckily, Darshana helped me see the error of my ways."

"Now that you're awake, I have to tell you what I saw." Mayhara pushed her dark hair out of her face. "It was some kind of graphics simulation in one of the conference rooms I stumbled upon last night."

Darshana took a seat in the chair across from her and folded her hands in her lap. "Go on."

"It was an animation of the comet." She grabbed her Linq from the coffee table and walked over to Darshana. She'd already played the video she'd recorded for Jae and the others while they'd drunk their tea, but if anyone might have more of a clue as to what the details of the video meant, it was Darshana.

Mayhara started the video and showed Darshana the screen. When the image of the comet hovered over the tunnel that led to a cavern, and the lines that must have represented some kind of vibration appeared on the screen, Darshana let out a *hmm*.

"Jae thinks it has something to do with Kashmeru's tomb," Mayhara said.

"I would guess the same." Darshana played the video again. She pointed to the bottom of the screen. "I don't seem to recognize any of the markings here. But if we can figure them out, we might have a better idea of where this is."

"Wait." Salina sat upright. "You mean you don't know where the tomb is?"

"It's been kept secret," Mr. Kitaro explained, stepping closer and tapping his fingers on his coffee cup. "Only the mages who sealed him in the tomb were aware of its location. The empire thought it best not to have the information public. Can you imagine the chaos it would create if it were common knowledge?"

"But this means the Pishacha—and the

government—know where it is."

"It's probably heavily guarded." Shiro rubbed at his chin. "Crawling with Pishacha, I'm sure."

"So when the comet is in the right position, they'll bring Naree there." Jae raked a hand through his hair.

"They're not going to be able to do anything if they don't have all seven daggers." Salina looked between Darshana and Mr. Kitaro. "Right?"

"That's the theory," Mr. Kitaro said.

They were quiet for a moment, but the silence was interrupted by a buzzing sound.

Jae pulled out his Linq, a wrinkle forming above his brows.

"What is it?" Mayhara asked.

"A message," he answered.

"From whom?" Darshana asked.

"Blocked ID," was all he said. And then he showed them his screen.

You'll find what you're looking for at the Danta Ramgarh Observatory

Eighteen

The car sped down the highway. Naree chewed on a nail while a battle raged in her head.

My love, please remember: they will try to deceive you. They will tell you our love isn't real. But it's the most real thing in the world. It has existed from the beginning of time and it will live on forever.

Naree closed her eyes and took a deep breath, trying to exhale her doubt.

They will try to make you believe I am using you. But only you know how I really feel. Only you understand how much I am devoted to you. Everything I have and everything I am is for you. Never forget that my love.

She put a hand on her heart. It swelled with memories from past lives, each of them filled with the existence of Kashmeru's love for her. Her body felt as if it were floating. Her skin tingled. Her mind cleared.

Never forget, my love.

"Never."

Nineteen

Salina parked the car and looked through the windshield at the observatory on the hill. The building was a standing silhouette in the twilight. The four mages stepped out of the car, none of them sure about what awaited them. Salina stretched out her legs, her nerves partially numb from long drive. She had asked to be the one to drive to keep her mind occupied with something other than the loss of her best friend. Heavy traffic had turned the two-hour journey into three hours of frustration.

"This mysterious message you got," Shiro said to Jae. "You think it was from the scroll makers?"

"That's what I thought at first." Jae adjusted the collar of his leather jacket. "Now I'm not so sure."

"Who else could it have been from?" Salina asked. "What was the message again?"

"Just that we'd find what we were looking for here."

"I don't know." Mayhara pulled the zipper of her jacket higher. "I've got a funny feeling about the whole thing."

As they continued toward the entrance of the observatory, Mayhara caught up with Salina. It wasn't the first time Mayhara had approached Salina like this in the past two days, checking to make sure she was all right. Though Salina hadn't come to terms with Huojin's death yet, she knew in her heart that she had to carry on with the mission, even doing so in Huojin's name.

"Hey." Mayhara bumped elbows with her. "You sure you're up for this?"

"Yes. I need to. Anything is better than obsessing over why Huojin was killed. It's time to put a stop to this before anyone else dies."

The observatory's lights were on, but no one could be seen inside. The glass doors at the entrance were locked, so Shiro pushed the call button. After what seemed like forever, a tall, thin woman with glasses and her reddish-brown hair in a bun came to the glass doors, studying them. She pressed the key code into the lock pad and gave them a polite smile.

"May I help you?"

Jae glanced at his friends. He couldn't very well say *we received a message to come here*, especially if this woman had no idea who they were or what they were looking for.

"Are you closed?" Salina asked.

The woman let out a small laugh. "This is a research observatory for scientists, not a public venue."

The mages exchanged glances. The message must not have come from this woman. But then, who was it from?

"Oh." Salina slapped a hand on Shiro's back, causing him to take a step forward. "Well, as luck would have it, Shiro here is a man of science. Isn't that right, Shiro?"

"We're part of his research team," Mayhara added. "Doing a paper on the Akutake comet."

"Uh, yes." Shiro fidgeted but then raised his chin,

giving off an air of confidence. "It's all very... scientific."

"Be that as it may, our protocol is for scientists to make an appointment beforehand." The woman flashed a fake smile, but she was clearly irritated. "Showing up out of the blue like this, especially at such a late hour, is highly unusual. Please call or use the website to make an appointment and I'd be happy to assist you."

She began to close the door.

"Please." Salina put her hand on the door. "You can make an exception, can't you?"

"I'm really sorry, but I can't. Goodbye now."

"Wait!" Mayhara said.

The woman ignored her and pushed the door harder to close it. Mayhara's palm glowed crimson, and suddenly a chunk of the floor in the doorway burst upward, creating a makeshift doorstop.

The woman's eyes grew wide, first fixated on the protrusion and then darting between the mages. She backed away. "No. No. I know who you are. Dark mages."

"No, we're not," Mayhara insisted.

"Of course you are. I've heard about you. Which one of you is the governor's son? Ha! Like I'd stick around to find out."

She turned to run.

Jae reached out with his sapphire magic as he called to her. "No, wait. You're mistaken. We are mages, but not dark ones. We're soldiers from the Empire of the Lotus."

His truth energy floated around her like blue sparkles as she stopped and turned to face him.

"You can trust us," Jae said, stepping into the building.

Salina, Shiro, and Mayhara followed close behind.

"I… I do," the woman said. "I don't know why I do, but, somehow, I know you're telling the truth."

"What's your name?" Jae asked.

"Asano."

"Asano, I'm guessing since you know about dark mages, you're also familiar with the Sacred Keys."

Shiro stepped closer. "She's one of them, isn't she?"

Asano looked to the blue glow of Jae's hands. "I am. I'm the keeper of one of the sacred daggers."

Salina and Mayhara exchanged glances, and then Mayhara drew closer.

"We need you to give it to us, Asano." Mayhara's

voice was gentle but even. "You're right to fear the dark mages. They're coming, and so are the Pishacha. It's just a matter of time before they find you and the dagger."

"But we can offer you protection," Jae added. "A hidden sanctuary and a safe place to hide the daggers."

"We'll have to move fast, though." Salina looked over her shoulder at the door, which was still propped open by Mayhara's floor bump. "Can you take us to the dagger?"

Asano wrung her hands and nodded. "Yes, of course. Follow me."

She led them from the lobby, up the metal stairs, and to the main observing floor. This floor, which was constructed of planks of metal grates, curved around the inside of the round building. The group passed a control room, which was filled with computers and other equipment, as well as a wall of monitors. One screen seemed to be devoted to monitoring solar flare activity, while another was focused on the Akutake comet. In the center of this building's level, the observatory's massive telescope stood like a colossal metal giant.

Asano brought the mages into a room that was lined with panels of dull gray, rectangular metal. Every panel looked the same, but Asano didn't even waver as she confidently approached one and pressed two pressure points. The panel slid out of the wall electronically like a small drawer, revealing a shelf holding a box.

Salina recognized the black-and-red object. She'd seen one just like it at the temple. It was the box that held a sacred dagger.

Asano used delicate movements as she retrieved the box. She blew out a shaky breath, presenting the box to Jae. Salina, Shiro, and Mayhara drew closer as Jae lifted the lid. They had to be sure the dagger was really inside.

Jae lifted the dagger and held it up to the light.

"We'll take that. Thanks." The voice came from behind them.

Salina turned, stunned to see a dark mage, flanked by two Pishacha in black mouth masks. The dark mage wore a long, dark gray cloak, and a loose, white, button-up shirt that exposed most of his chest. His hair was buzzed short on the sides, the remaining dark hair pulled back into a ponytail. One of his eyebrows had slashes in it, as if the hairs had been cut with a razor.

"No!" Salina immediately crouched and shot off a blast of fire at the intruders. The dark mage covered his face from the flame. As soon as the wave of heat died off, he extended his arms. All the metal in the room warped, including the floor. Asano and the mages stumbled. Stunned by the unexpected move, Mayhara had to take a second before she could reach out and stabilize the mages' balance.

In that instant, Asano grabbed the dagger from Jae and spun away. Her movements were so calculated, they were almost too fast to catch as she darted for a section of the wall indistinguishable from any other section. But this one had a secret doorway she slipped through, and in an instant, she was gone, and the door was shut.

"Mayhara! Shiro!" Jae shouted. "Go after her. Salina and I will handle these guys."

"Yeah, come *handle* us," the dark mage taunted. "Give us a chance to get rid of another one of you."

Everything seemed to happen at once.

Mayhara and Shiro ran to the wall, pressing random spots in the damaged metal in hopes of finding the secret pressure point to release the hidden door.

Salina filled with rage at the dark mage's words and threw her arms forward, blasting the enemy with a horizontal cyclone of fire. The dark mage and Pishacha backed into the hall to shield themselves.

Salina and Jae then charged into the hall. The enemy had spread out, moving steadily, as if they were predators stalking their prey. Their heavy, black boots scraped across the metal floor as they advanced.

Jae lifted his chin and shifted closer to Salina. "Cover your ears," he said to her.

She did as he'd commanded. Jae raised his glowing palms and slapped them together hard, creating a huge blast of sound. The waves tore through the air and forced the Pishacha and the dark mage back. The dark mage crashed into the side of the telescope. The Pishacha disappeared into clouds of black smoke before they collided with the metal equipment situated around the floor.

Taking advantage of their enemies' struggles, Jae and Salina ran for the stairs.

"Mayhara and Shiro are gone," Jae said as they raced for the door.

"They must have figured out how to get through that secret passage," Salina said. "It has to lead outside somehow. That's the only thing that makes sense."

Just as they reached the entrance to the building, the Pishacha reappeared in front of them. One of them unfolded his black cloak to reveal the dark mage, who stepped out with a sneer. They must have grabbed him with their magic and brought him with them.

With a cry of rage, Salina threw her hand out. A long whip of golden fire extended from her palm. She flailed it out, the end of it whipping at their enemies. Smoke appeared as the Pishacha disappeared again. The dark mage hissed as he recoiled from the whip.

"I hear them." Jae lunged forward and out the door. "They're across the cliff."

Salina sprinted behind him, trusting his power of sound to track Asano and their friends. She heaved each breath as her feet pounded the ground. Overhead, the sky had darkened to night. Only the moon lit their way over the uneven surface of the cliff.

At last they spotted Mayhara and Shiro running not far from the edge of the cliff. Asano was a small distance in front of them, and Mayhara was shouting for her to stop.

"You tricked me!" Asano screamed. "You used some kind of magic on me to make me believe you're on the side of the Lotus."

"No, that's not true." Mayhara was fast, closing the

distance between them. "We *are* on the side of the Lotus."

Jae's palms glowed blue, but Salina could see the others were too far away for his truth powers to work.

"Please, stop!" Shiro yelled.

Mayhara grunted, her palms glowing red. She aimed for the ground by Asano's feet. In the next second, Asano stumbled and fell forward. The dagger flew from her fingers, skidding across the dirt and landing inches away from the cliff's edge.

"No!" Asano scrambled to her feet and jumped for the dagger. She stood, shaking, with the dagger in her hand.

"Asano." Jae held his hands up in a peaceful gesture, his palms still glowing blue. "We are with the empire. We are telling you the truth. We don't want to hurt you."

Asano breathed heavily, but her features softened. The wind whipped her hair around her head as she kept her eyes on Jae. After what seemed like forever, she nodded.

"Okay. I believe you." Asano took a step forward, but the earth fell away at her feet. Her eyes widened and her mouth went agape as she dropped.

A scream as loud as thunder erupted from Mayhara

as she raced forward, crimson energy tearing through the air toward Asano.

The mages rushed to the edge of the cliff. When they got there, they could see a small section of rock jutting out from the cliffside. The dagger had landed on it, but Asano was clinging to it by her fingertips. Debris fell from the rock where her fingers held on.

"Save the Lotus," Asano said, her voice quavering.

Jae dropped to his chest to reach down for her, but her fingers slipped away then, and she plummeted down. The mages could only stare, their hearts hammering in their chests, as the Sacred Key disappeared into the darkness below.

Twenty

Jae closed his eyes and dropped his head to the ground, his heart aching for the woman who'd just fallen to her death. There was nothing they could have done to save her. Mayhara had tried, but her efforts had been in vain. Jae stayed on the ground for a moment, coming to terms with what had just happened. He could hear the other mages get to their feet behind him, but for the moment, he couldn't move.

"Jae," Mayhara said. There was something in her voice that set off alarms in his head.

He lifted his chin and pushed out his hearing powers. There were footsteps. It sounded like a lot of people approaching.

His eyes landed on the dagger, but he didn't pick it up. Perhaps it was best to leave it there for now. He turned and got to his feet, following the gazes of the other mages. They were approaching—the Pishacha, the dark mages… and Naree.

His eyes locked with hers as she stomped up the hill, flanked by two dark mages. In front of her were the two Pishacha from the observatory, their coal-black eyes boring into each of the mages, one after the other. Jae searched Naree's face, trying to see some remaining clue of the sister he'd grown up with, the sister he'd do anything for. But she simply sneered back at him with a hatred in her eyes that shook him to the core.

"Naree. We're not here to fight you," Jae said. "Not again. We want you to come with us. We are *your* army."

The dark mage beside her— the one from the observatory—laughed, casting a glance at his fellow dark mages. "We are her army now. She has Kashmeru. She has no need for you any longer."

"Naree," Jae said, ignoring the dark mage. His palms glowed blue, reaching out to her with his truth powers. "Please, listen to your soul. Even as Lakshmi, you must know this isn't right. We can help you, get you back on track to doing what's right."

There was a blue glow in her palms as well. Her expression didn't change. It was as if she hadn't heard him at all. Naree stretched out her shoulders. "What is it you hope to achieve? I'm not here to be saved. Kashmeru has promised me peace, an eternity with him, a life beyond the destruction of the universe. You can't stop destiny. Kashmeru and I were made for each other, to be the ultimate gods, together. Forever."

"Naree," Jae pleaded. "Kashmeru is lying to you. You were meant to rule, but in pure love and peace, not in the dredges of his evil ways."

Naree shook her head. "Kashmeru told me you would try to manipulate me, to feed me lies. I won't fall for it. You are nothing to me."

The words stung, but Jae knew deep down that it wasn't his sister saying these things. Her mind was poisoned by an evil god. There had to be a way to win her back.

"Fine." Naree crossed her arms and raised a brow. "You don't want to fight? Give me the daggers."

Jae slowly shook his head. "You know I can't do that."

She let out a laugh he wasn't familiar with—another indication that his sister wasn't herself. "And *you* know I'll get them one way or another. You have one right now, don't you? Where is it?"

The glow in her palms turned from blue to purple. She was pushing out her power of insight, trying to get the location of the dagger. Jae wasn't sure his power over lies would hide it from her.

"We don't have it," Shiro said, stepping in beside Jae. "And even if we did, we'd do anything to prevent you and your crew of lackies from getting it."

"You think you intimidate me. How cute." Naree looked from Shiro to Salina to Mayhara to Jae. "You honestly believe it will be a problem for me to defeat all four of you at once?"

"What about eight?"

The voice seemed to come out of nowhere. It made Naree, the Pishacha, and the three dark mages turn around searching for its source.

Stepping out of the shadow of night and into the moonlight were four mages. Jae only recognized two of them, but he knew they all must have been on their side. The purple, green, blue, and white glow of their palms gave him hope.

Mayhara shifted closer to Jae. "Elites?" she whispered.

Jae's eyes drifted to her for only a moment as he nodded.

The mage who'd spoken up held her hands open at her sides, her palms alit with purple.

The amethyst mage.

She had thick black hair that hung in loose waves. Even from as far away as she was standing, Jae could see the flecks of purple in her eyes. She wasn't one of the ones he recognized, but she appeared to be the leader. The ones he did remember from the academy were Loni, the emerald mage, and Kamal, the sapphire mage. Loni looked the same as when he'd last seen her, except perhaps thinner, as if she hadn't been eating properly. And her straight, dark hair had grown to way below her shoulders. Kamal appeared taller than when Jae had last seen him, but he still sported stringy black hair that hung in his face. The auburn-haired girl whose palms glowed white was not a familiar face, but because she looked so young, he assumed this diamond mage hadn't been at the academy long before the Eradication.

Could these be the elites? What were the chances that they'd all found each other and shown up exactly when Jae and his friends needed them?

Naree looked between them, her breaths heavy as she considered what to do.

The amethyst mage stepped around Naree and her group, the other mages following her until they were next to Jae and the others. The Pishacha and the dark mages kept their eyes on them, their jaws squared and their fists clenched, ready to do as Naree commanded.

"You may have us outnumbered," Naree said, "but that doesn't mean you can overpower us."

Naree nodded to the three dark mages. The one from the observatory held out his palms. The air around them seemed to vibrate. Shiro gasped as his feet slid forward, as if he were being pulled by an invisible force. Mayhara rushed forward, stepping in front of Shiro to stop his movement, and held her palms up at the dark mage. Crimson energy flew from her palms, and the earth beneath the dark mage trembled. He crouched down and slapped his hands on the ground to keep his balance.

Naree sneered. "Destroy them!"

Chaos erupted as particles of energy flew back and forth between the two sides. Air whipped through the enemy, knocking them back a few feet, but they soon recovered and sent shockwaves of pain at the elite mages and Jae, causing them to cry out. It was as if their bones were being crushed.

The diamond mage grunted through the pain and stepped forward, throwing out her hands. Blinding white light emitted from her palms and formed a shimmering, curved shield over the elites and Jae. The shockwaves stopped, the energy bouncing off the diamond mage's shield.

One of the Pishacha disappeared from beside Naree and reappeared on the elite's side of the shield. He jumped into the air in a flying kick and planted the heel of his left boot into Jae's chest. The momentum knocked Jae hard on his back. As Jae rolled to the side to get back on his feet, Salina grabbed the shadow soldier by his cloak and pushed him over the edge of the cliff. He disappeared into a cloud of black smoke before he had a chance to fall.

The other Pishacha sneered as he tried his turn, disappearing and then reappearing on the mages' side of the shield. But Shiro manifested blocks of ice around the Pishacha's legs, sealing him in place as Mayhara slammed into him with two hammering fists. The blows knocked him backward. As he collided with the hard ground, he made his smoky exit.

Naree's eyes glowed as she raised her hands. A white light to match the elite diamond mage's poured from her palms and shot toward the diamond shield. The shimmering diamond energy from both sides rammed into each other, emitting a high-pitched screeching sound like metal scraping metal. Naree kept pushing, trying to penetrate the shield, but it was too strong.

"Kamal," the amethyst mage called. "Mute us!"

Kamal's blue glow expanded until it stretched farther than the diamond mage's bubble. He nodded to the amethyst mage.

"Do you have the dagger?" she asked Jae.

"It's near," he answered.

"You're going to have to grab it on my signal, and then we need to hurry down the hill. You have a sanctuary?"

"Yes. You can follow us there."

"We won't have much time. I can only hold them off for so long."

Jae nodded, then cast a glance at Shiro, Mayhara, and Salina. They each nodded in agreement.

"Now!" the amethyst mage yelled.

The diamond mage dropped her shield. The amethyst mage held her arms out in front of her and aimed her palms at the Pishacha and dark mages. Purple crystals pushed out into the air toward them. Loni, the emerald mage, blasted out air to hold them back while the purple cloud of energy reached them.

With a wild scream, Naree dropped to her knees, covering her eyes. The dark mages flailed and thrashed, eventually dropping to the ground as well.

Sight. The amethyst mage had temporarily blinded them.

Jae didn't hesitate. He bent down, reached past the cliff's edge, and seized the dagger, thankful it was still there. "Let's go!"

Naree threw out air, fire, earth, ice, and blaring sound, attempting to stop the elites, but she could not find them. The elites and Jae raced down the hill, keeping their balance thanks to Mayhara's energy. The steep slope aided their progress, and soon they were at their car.

"You have a car?" Jae asked the amethyst mage.

"It's hidden around the corner. Meet us there and we'll follow you. The blindness will wear off soon, so we need to hurry."

"What's your name?" Jae asked her.

"It's Apinya. But everyone calls me Penny." Penny pointed to the other mages. "You know Kamal and Loni. This is Yuki."

Jae nodded his greeting to them. Jae and Loni only looked at each other for a moment before averting their gazes.

"I'm Mayhara," Mayhara said before pointing to rest. "Salina and Shiro."

"I don't mean to be rude," Salina said, "but we don't have time to be social right now. We've got to go."

"She's right," Kamal said. "Time for chitchat later. They're going to be coming for us, and they're already beyond pissed."

"We'll follow you," Penny said.

"Wait." Jae put a hand on Penny's arm. "Were you the one who sent the message with this location?"

"Yes," Penny said. "I knew the dagger was here."

"How?" Jae asked.

"I know where all the daggers are. I'll tell you more when we reach your sanctuary."

Jae could only stare for a moment, watching as she hurried to her vehicle. She knew where the daggers were. The odds might have just changed to be in their favor. He was still wrapping his head around it as he turned to get into the car, but the purple haze at the top of the hill caught his eye.

Naree.

She was up there. Part of him wanted to rush back up and grab her, force her to come with them. But it was too risky. And she would fight him. Clenching his jaw, Jae hit a fist against the top of the car, then swung the door open to climb inside, hoping he'd still get a chance to save his little sister.

The story continues in

Emerald Mage

TURN THE PAGE
FOR A
PREVIEW OF
EMERALD MAGE,
BOOK FOUR
IN THE
EMPIRE OF THE LOTUS
SERIES

One

Joni Saengkaew stared at the emerald stone on her wristband as the car climbed a hidden road headed uphill. The stone caught the light of the moon, reminding her of the many nights she'd spent fearing the fulfillment of the prophecy. Things had been a mess since the destruction of the academy, but the last few months, in particular, had turned her life upside down. She sucked in a sharp breath through her nose and crossed her arms, clenching her hands into fists and tucking them in at her sides

In the driver's seat, Penny spared her a glance, the flecks of purple in her eyes sparkling from the street lights. Out of the four mages in the car, she and Penny had been together the longest, venturing as a team through the post-Eradication chaos to get to where they were now.

Loni had been squatting in an abandoned Linq factory for almost three months when Penny had found her. It was just one of the many places she had camped out while on the run. Penny had simply shown up, in her dark purple leather jacket and knee-high, black boots, telling Loni she needed to come with her. Thankfully, Loni had remembered Penny from the academy, but they hadn't been in touch in years, so it had been a surprise to see her. As the elite Amethyst mage, Penny had used her power of insight to find her, but because Loni had moved around so much, she hadn't been easy to track down. And Loni hadn't even known at the time that she was the elite. Apparently, the station had been passed down when the current emerald elite had been found dead in the prison camps. Penny said it had been murder.

The trees flanking the small road they were driving on began to decrease in number. Up ahead, at the top of the hill, the surroundings cleared to reveal a beautiful temple. Loni leaned forward and took in a deep breath, as if inhaling the sacredness of the temple, hoping for comfort. The truth was she was a wreck inside. Physically, mentally, and, most of all, emotionally. The only thing keeping her going was justice. She'd promised herself she would see this through. She would destroy Kashmeru herself, if she could.

The car in front of them—the one they'd been following—pulled into a carport. Another car was already parked there, along with a motorcycle that she recognized.

When they parked, Loni looked over at Yuki—the diamond mage—who removed a hairband from her wrist and swept up her shoulder-length, auburn hair into a messy bun. Yuki yawned, and Loni almost made a joke about it being past her bedtime but refrained. Yuki had heard it all before. At seventeen, she was probably the youngest elite mage to have ever existed.

The four mages emerged from the car simultaneously. Kamal—the elite sapphire mage—stretched his arms above his head and slightly arched his back. As he kicked out his long legs, he looked around at his driving companions, his ever-present, cocky grin twisting his lips to one side.

The four passengers from the other car were already waiting for them. Jae—whom Loni knew well—signaled for them to follow and headed toward a door seemingly guarded by a white, stone elephant. He looked almost the same as she'd remembered, with his short, dark, hero hair and his square shoulders. He did seem a little more worn for the wear, but the rugged look suited him.

For being so close to the busy road at the bottom of the hill, the temple was quieter than Loni had expected. She had to admit, though, that the pink sandstone columns and white marble floors were a far more pleasing aesthetic than the murky, soiled, and rotten-egg-scented places she'd been used to camping out in during the past couple of years.

Up ahead of her, the crimson mage—Mayhara, she remembered—ran her hand along one of the stone elephants' tusks before she entered the temple door. There was no denying she was beautiful. Her flawless creamed-caramel skin contrasted nicely with her thick, dark hair. Jae placed a hand on the small of Mayhara's back as he followed her inside. Loni wondered, with an itch of jealousy, how long they'd been a couple.

"Come on inside." Shiro—the copper mage—held up the dagger, which he'd wrapped in a red cloth. "I'm going to store this somewhere safe and catch up with you."

Inside, the temple's ceilings were at least ten feet high, and the marble floors were polished. It didn't feel like a temple. The feeling Loni got was more like it was an extravagant home, filled with comfortable furniture. Though, she wasn't too familiar with many homes decorated with elegant stone statues of various deities. A gentle breeze floated in behind the mages as they entered the building, carrying with it the pleasant scent of jasmine.

An archway to the right of the main entrance hallway led them to a spacious kitchen. In the breakfast nook, sitting at a small black ceramic table, were two older people. Loni recognized the woman as Darshana, her guru from the academy. The man, however, she'd never seen before.

Darshana eyed the group coming in and jumped to

her feet. Her hands flew to her mouth, trembling slightly. Her white hair was pulled back into the long braid Loni was familiar with, and she still had stunning skin for someone her age.

"I can't believe it." Darshana walked over to the four new mages and took each of them by their hands, one after the other. One by one, they bowed to her in greeting.

The salt-and-pepper-haired man at the table stood. Loni had expected him to be taller than he was, probably due to the sense of importance he seemed to convey. He certainly dressed like someone important. He bowed as he approached them. "Judging by the amount of jovial energy flooding the room, I assume these are the other elites we have been looking for. It's a pleasure to meet you. I am Mr. Kitaro."

"He's a Sacred Key," Jae explained. "A keeper of one of the magic daggers."

"Cool," Kamal said, flipping the bangs of his stringy black hair with a jerk of his head.

Jae raised a brow at his comment, causing Loni to bite the inside of her cheek to keep from laughing.

"I'm Apinya. But everyone calls me 'Penny.'" Penny

bowed to Mr. Kitaro.

"Ah. *Apinya*." Mr. Kitaro nodded. "It means 'magical powers.' How fitting. You have wonderful specks of purple in your irises, matching your amethyst mage powers. How perfect."

Penny's forehead creased for a fraction of a second. "Thank you?"

Next to her, Kamal bowed again while sticking his hands in his pockets, typically combining an air of respect and apathy in one move. "I'm Kamal, and I guess I'm the new elite sapphire mage. Penny just found me a week ago to let me know, so I'm still trying to wrap my head around it."

"Nice to meet you, Kamal," Mr. Kitaro said.

Since she stood beside Kamal, Loni decided to go next. She raised her hand and then stuck it behind her back. "I'm Loni. Emerald elite."

"One of my best friends from childhood was an emerald mage." While Mr. Kitaro smiled, it didn't reach his eyes.

Loni refrained from questioning whether or not that friend was still alive.

Everyone's gaze then went to Yuki. She looked

around with her wide eyes as if unsure of what to do. Relief seemed to wash over her when Penny spoke up for her.

"Yuki is the diamond elite."

"I should probably be shocked by such a young elite," Mr. Kitaro said. "But diamond mages are so rare that I imagine the former elites who were... *eliminated* by the Pishacha were few in number."

Yuki's only response was to drop her gaze as she nodded, tendrils of her long, auburn hair slipping from her hairband and falling in front of her pale, narrow face.

"You all look famished," Mr. Kitaro said.

"I'll make more tea," Darshana said, heading for the stove and grabbing the kettle to fill.

Kamal raked a hand through his hair. "I mean, I could use a shower and a beer if we're offering things."

"Why don't I whip up something to eat?" Jae's gaze fell upon Loni before he headed for the cupboards.

"I'll help," Mayhara said. Her smile told Loni she hadn't caught the look Jae had just given her.

Though Loni couldn't be sure what meaning might have been behind that look in the first place. Because the last look he'd ever given her had been one of disappointment.

They'd moved into the dining room so everyone could sit comfortably around the table and eat. Penny moved her food around her plate but hadn't taken a bite. Though the *bibim gooksu* Jae and Mayhara had whipped up smelled delicious, with the scent of spices and vinegar filling the air, Penny simply had too much to divulge to the group and was in no rush to eat.

"So you saw my Linq number in your head?" Jae asked, reaching for the water carafe to fill his glass. "I didn't know amethyst mages could do that."

"Normally, we can't," Penny said.

"It's a highly unusual skill," Darshana added.

"Good thing, too." Kamal snorted. "Otherwise, amethysts everywhere would be stealing credit account numbers and winning lotteries on the fly."

Yuki gave him a disapproving look.

"It took a lot of meditation," Penny said, ignoring Kamal's remark. "And when I finally pinned it down, I contacted you right away."

"Via a mysterious message." Salina pointed her chopsticks at Darshana. "Which actually led us to one of the daggers."

Penny shrugged. "I figured it would be diligent to kill two birds with one stone. Plus, I didn't want to identify myself in the message, just in case it was intercepted."

"Which it might have been," Mayhara said. "Would explain why the Pishacha showed up."

"So you know where the other daggers are, then." Shiro narrowed his eyes as if he were trying to calculate some major mathematical equation.

"Yes." Penny set down her chopsticks. "The Pishacha have three of them."

Shiro almost choked, sputtering as he tried to clear his throat. "Three? I thought they only had two."

"Yeah, we counted two," Salina added.

"One was acquired recently." Penny dropped her gaze, as if disappointed in herself. "They got to it before we could."

Darshana put a hand on her chest, taking a deep breath. "Yes. Yes, you are right. I'd felt a disturbance, but I believed it to be Huojin's downfall."

Salina frowned. Penny could feel Salina's sorrow over her friend's demise as if it were her own loss.

Mr. Kitaro bowed his head and closed his eyes. "Another Sacred Key has fallen."

It was quiet for a moment. And then Mayhara spoke up. "They have three, and we have three. There's one left. You know where it is?"

Penny nodded. "I do."

A tingling sensation traveled in a repeating wave through Penny's head. Her senses were on high alert. Someone was approaching the temple.

"We should probably—" Jae stopped mid-sentence when Penny abruptly turned her head and stood from the table.

As she proceeded from the dining room toward the front door, she could hear the others following her.

"Penny," Loni called. "Should we be afraid?"

Penny didn't stop walking, her boots clunking along on the marble floor in a consistent rhythm. "I'm not sure. Something is wrong, but I can't tell."

Searching her mind, she found something blocking her insight powers. It had to be magic; that was the only thing that made sense. But what was it? She could just make out the faint glow of the various-colored light behind her as the other mages prepared themselves for a possible fight. But Penny couldn't sense that they were in any danger. Unless her senses were betraying her.

She opened the door.

There, not ten feet from where she was standing, was a young woman with smooth, pale skin and dark, unkempt hair hobbling toward the door. On one arm, she propped up an older woman with scraggly white hair.

"Amalia?" Darshana said from behind Penny. Her eyes were on the older woman.

"Help," the young woman said. "She's dying."

READ MORE OF EMERALD MAGE

AVAILABLE NOW!

From Snowy Wings Publishing

http://books2read.com/EmeraldMage

In case you missed it…

Be sure to check out book one and two in the

Empire of the Lotus series:

Available from all online retailers

CRIMSON MAGE

http://books2read.com/crimsonmage

and

COPPER MAGE

http://books2read.com/coppermage

Acknowledgements

It's a weird world. I edited this book during the COVID-19 pandemic, when the actual real world felt like a dystopian film in the making. At the time of writing these acknowledgements, the pandemic is not over yet, and I've been "cooped up" in my house with my family for the past three weeks. Though it's a scary time, if I look on the bright side, it gave me more time to work on this series. So, I'm not thanking the virus, but I am thankful for the time.

As usual, thanks to all my friends and family who have supported me and my books through the years. My ARC team, my agent, my writing buddies. This is why I continue to write.

A special thanks goes out to Winta Ketema, who graciously assisted me with all things Eritrea. Thanks so much, Winta. You're a star!

And thank you, Kirsten, for another awesome cover!

ABOUT THE AUTHOR

Dorothy Dreyer is a Philippine-born American living in Germany with her husband, her two college kids, and two Siberian Huskies. She is an award-winning, *USA Today* Bestselling Author of young adult and new adult books that usually have some element of magic or the supernatural in them. Aside from reading, she enjoys movies, binge-watching series, chocolate, take-out, traveling, and having fun with friends and family.

You can find out more about Dorothy on her website: http://dorothydreyer.com

www.ingramcontent.com/pod-product-compliance
Lightning Source LLC
Chambersburg PA
CBHW050523190726
48284CB00003B/921